OUR HEAVEN   1

Our HEAVEN

A PENDLETON PREP NOVEL

H.L. PACKER

DEDICATION

To Vicki,
I hope this makes up for the end of Their Hell!

READER NOTE

Please note, The Sect, Her Devil, His Angel, and Their Hell should be read ahead of this story. The Sect is available for free here: https://dl.bookfunnel.com/t4aqupbw3, Her Devil is on all retailers: https://books2read.com/HerDevil as is His Angel: https://books2read.com/His-Angel and Their Hell; https://books2read.com/theirHell

Copyright

Copyright © 2024 HL Packer

All rights reserved. Without limiting the rights under copyright reserved above, no part of this publication may be reproduced, stored in or introduced into retrieval system, or transmitted, in any form, or by any means (electronic, mechanical, photocopying, recording or otherwise) without the prior written permission of both the copyright owner and the above publisher of this book.

This is a work of fiction. Names, characters, places, brands, media, and incidents are either the products of the author's imagination or are used fictitiously. The author acknowledges the trademark owners of various products referenced in this work of fiction, which have been used without permission. The publication/use of these trademarks is not authorised, associated with, or sponsored by the trademark owners.

Editor – Vicki at The Indie Hub

Cover Designer – LJDesigns

Formatter – LJDesigns

RECAP, TIME!

So, very briefly for those of you who read the first stories a little while ago and aren't bingeing the entire series in one fell swoop, let's recap.

Ivy had a fall out with her father when he demanded she put off her dreams of going away to university to become a psychologist in order to attend Pendleton Prep for a year. It wasn't up for negotiation, but she got to take her best friend Tamsin along for the ride.

Tamsin is a touch more free-spirited than Ivy and is determined to make the most of a year away from their parents overbearing supervision to enjoy her freedom. When they arrived, they found that instead of standard accommodation, they'd been upgraded and are now in a pool house with four other girls and, despite a few challenges, they get on well.

They meet a bunch of guys at a mixer event and get invited to a party at their place—whispers of some secret fraternity being thrown around, when dresses and an official invitation arrive for them.

It turns out the guys they met at the mixer live at the big stone house in front of theirs, and are, in fact, part of some secret society called The Sect. They're all introduced to a bunch of masked members before the party, then the girls are raised up above everyone else through a fun evening of entertainment.

Things aren't quite as straight forward for the guys, though. They end up being dragged out of bed after the mixer event and are made to clean up the campus as part of their challenge criteria. They're put on a drink restriction and given a few other simple rules before being told how important the Angels are. Yep, they're the girls that live in the pool house.

A bunch of guys being trapped in a house with no way to burn off steam means that Nick and Jacob end up sparring. When that goes too far for other people, Nick storms off, only for Ivy to find him half beaten and bleeding on the driveway.

The adrenaline does a number on both their inhibitions when she realises he's okay, and they end up getting hot and heavy in the woods before going back to the pool house. The girls begin their peer training for a Big Sister project, and George is removed from the competition. A few days later, they find out someone has targeted Stephanie.

Oliver rallies the Devils and makes an example of him, only for Nick and Wyatt to realise how exposed Ivy is, and they formulate a plan to keep her safe. Unfortunately, that plan doesn't go quite how they intended, and she ends up terrified but tied to Nick.

Tamsin decides to link herself with Taylor, and Leo and Jacob finally get together, before Nick demands time with Ivy after she gives him the silent treatment. They come to some kind of peace, and he helps formulate a plan to help win over her Little Sister.

The Angels host a pamper afternoon, and Ivy runs into Wyatt, who then turns up with some of the guys as 'shirtless butlers' for the afternoon. Not to be outdone, Nick and the rest of the guys (in their jealousy) crash the party, and the massages become a little less than professional.

The guys are pulled into another challenge—this one a series of escape rooms. Jacob almost gets hit with a dagger, Wyatt nearly ends up trapped with a killer, and Emmerson leaves the competition, then they're down to seven.

With everything getting so serious, they decide another party is in order. Tamsin and Taylor mirror themselves together, and Ivy finally starts to make progress with her Little Sister Ruby. They're all called in by The Sect to celebrate the new couple, only they're then removed from the competition because of broken rules.

Devastated, Ivy relies on the guys to hold her together through her grief, and the five of them find some kind of safety together, amongst other things. Leo and Wyatt try to tie themselves together, but they get interrupted, and it never gets finished when Nick begins to pull away.

As the girls begin to fight within themselves for position and power, Ivy decides a declaration needs to be made and gathers everyone together to make sure they know the Devils are off limits, while Leo puts in place a backup plan just as Nick disappears.

Luckily for him, they manage to get him back before any permanent damage is done – with a little help from Leo's father, and some serious standing up for themselves, but it doesn't come without a warning to Leo's brothers.

Unfortunately, Nick starts to sink into himself, feeling like he failed them, and an argument ensues between Wyatt and Leo, with Jacob kicking them both in the right direction. This division spurs Ivy on to set boundaries between them, swearing a blood oath to each other to love, care for, and protect each other, until death.

The guys do their best to support Nick in his recovery, getting him up and moving, pulling him out of the depths of the depression he'd been slowly sinking into, while Ivy continues to build bridges with Ruby.

Something Ruby says triggers a memory for Leo and, suspicious, he watches and waits, seeing what could only be one of his brothers collecting her from their shopping trip, and then they're pulled into a challenge, Stephanie tagging along as the only mirrored Angel.

Sadly, Jasper is the one who doesn't come back. After a close call with Jacob and some miscommunication on return, the group take solace together, Aimee taking comfort with Penelope and Charlotte.

Wyatt has an awakening moment with Leo, followed up by a conversation with Nick, and as a group, Ivy, Charlotte, Penelope, Jacob, Wyatt, Leo and Nick put the trees up and decorate the house ready for Christmas.

Leo has a not-so-warm welcome when he returns home on Christmas Eve, finding the house already halfway through a party, and a young girl being abused in his name. Keeping her safe, he drops her home the following morning before having a run in with his father's second in command.

He gets an apartment key from his father and finds out that Ruby is more important than he realised, somehow linked to his brother Dex, whilst Blaise is being trained up to become his second-in-command, when the time inevitably comes.

Ballgowns arrive at the house, and all the Devils and Angels are expected at a New Year's party, new masks in tow, but when they get there the boys are pulled into a

challenge. Jacob doesn't make it out, and when the boys
eventually return to the ballroom, the girls are missing too.

ONE

Ivy

Do you know *what it feels like to find all your hopes and dreams shattered on the floor around you? No, I bet you don't, and I'm very sorry for whatever happened if you do.*

It didn't come like a black knight on a steed, not seen from the distance, not swift. It was a series of events that slowly but surely unfurled, chipping away at my life, my confidence, at my very sense of self. But I'm jumping ahead. Let me fill in a few blanks for you.

The band plays, the music soft, lilting, traditional, and old, much like the ballroom we're currently standing in. The Devils are still nowhere to be seen. Stephanie is growing more and more agitated as the moments tick by, but we all know there's nothing we can do except wait.

Aimee and I loiter at the edge of the dance floor, with her keeping an eye on the doors, and me watching the dancers twirl around and around, hoping one of them is going to turn out to be our Devils. Just busy, not lost.

I feel the heat of him before he speaks; a silent warning cascading across my skin. "Is your partner not around?" he asks, the man with the green mask—the one from earlier on—while Aimee eyes him with interest.

"I'm not linked to a Devil, and they appear to have found themselves a little indisposed at the moment," I reply, watching the dancers and doing my best to ignore his strong presence at my side. You can't trust anyone here.

It's confidence more than anything. An understanding of his place in this world, in this room.

He's here for a reason.

Intentional. It's all so intentional.

"That's a shame, but there's no reason for you ladies to miss out on the event. Can I interest either of you in a dance?"

The question is innocuous enough, and yet everyone here came with a partner, and his wife interrupted our dance earlier on. *Do we really need to be adding any more problems onto this evening?*

"Does your wife not mind you spending your evening dancing with the young, single Angels rather than her?" I ask, just as she twirls past us with a new partner of her own. "I guess not."

I'd been doing so well. Sipping the champagne, watching the dancing, doing my best to pretend this beautiful, seventeenth century reenactment in the most amazing venue I've ever seen is real, but it's not. It's just another front. A facade for The Sect. A way to get us all here and force the men I care about to fight their way through whatever ridiculous things they have planned. Again. More and more, I'm seeing it—the sickness behind the beauty.

Penelope and Stephanie smile as they pass, their

interested gazes lingering on the man at my side. *It's a shame not everyone is as disenchanted as I am.*

"It would be rude to leave my friend alone."

"It's fine," Aimee says, brushing me off. "I'm going to go and check on Charlotte, anyway. She's been way too long in the bathroom."

Hopefully she's not passed out, or worse. Sadly, she found someone here willing to hand over more of that white powder she loves so much. Sure, a bump or two at a party is fun, and it's helped with the all-night revision sessions from time to time, but I'm well aware of the fine line between recreation and addiction.

"Shall we?" the man asks, offering his hand.

"I don't even know your name."

"You need to know my name to dance?" he asks with curiosity, and I can almost picture the dark, raised eyebrow hiding behind the mask. "It's Thomas, but most people just call me Tom."

"Nice to meet you, Thomas. I'm Ivy."

I turn and take his outstretched hand once Aimee walks away, letting him guide me to the dance floor, even though the music is now sultrier than it was as the evening devolves from something polite to something… else.

"I know who you are, little Angel," he whispers, pulling me in so my chest presses against his in an unexpected move of power.

It should come as a surprise that he knows who I am, but it doesn't, and if he was going for the shock factor, it falls flat on its perfect face.

"That's a beautiful necklace," he comments, spinning

me to the side before drawing me back in again.

"Thank you. It was a gift." My fingers itch to touch it, to run across its smooth surface and remember the peace and safety Wyatt promised it would provide, but they're held captive by the man in front of me as he guides us carefully through the throng of dancers.

"From a Devil?"

I nod as he pushes me away, twirling me out, no further explanation required as awareness prickles over my skin. I should have anticipated that we were being watched, but this feels different—a bristle of something ominous loitering in the wings.

"And yet you're not paired with one," he muses, snapping me back in and reminding me that there's more than just the Devils under scrutiny here.

I have no doubt he knows exactly which Devils I'm intertwined with, and exactly how that looks to the rest of the world. The Sect knows all, or so they continue to remind us. After all, if he knows who I am despite the mask, it only stands to reason that he knows who everyone else is and where we each fit into this puzzle.

"You must have them wrapped around your little finger," he muses.

"So, that's why you're here, is it? To try and work out what's so beguiling about the Angel that's got four of your Devils tangled up?"

"Four? I thought two of them were wrapped up in each other," he says, the music changing again to a tango. He switches the hold effortlessly, the push and pull so close to the war with words we're engaged in, it's almost fitting.

"It's a little more complicated than that," I reply, my hand on his chest before I attempt to step away.

My mind runs at a mile a minute, desperately attempting to appear cool, calm, and collected, despite the conversation at hand. Me walking away could be part of the dance, and nobody watching would be any wiser, but all this talk about the Devils has fear racing through my veins.

Where are they? When will they be back? How many of them will come back?

Just when I think I'm free and he's going to let me walkaway, Thomas grabs my hand, pulling me back in against his body, but it's not the refuge I'd like it to be.

This hot, slightly older guy—the one that 'wanted to make sure we were having a good night'—knows way too much, and he feels like a threat. Suddenly, every move feels off, and every comment seems poignant. *So much for wanting to make sure we have an enjoyable evening.*

Why was he asking those questions earlier on? What I wanted from life, what my hopes and dreams were. How does all that mix in with the Devils or The Sect, and what use could it be to him? Because it's going to be used for something at some point, that much is inevitable.

After turning me under his arm, he pushes me out before pulling me back in, the movement constant, the tango frustrating for more than just the dance moves.

"So I'm beginning to understand," he says. "Shall we get a drink?"

I nod, grateful for the opportunity to carve some space between us as he tips his head, offers his arm, and moves us away from the dance floor. Rather than plucking a glass from one of the passing waitresses, though, he heads towards the back of the room and the bar. Only as we near, he passes, heads towards the entranceway, and holds the door for me.

"I thought we were getting a drink?"

The bar is right there, lots of people are, too, but for some reason, he's taking us away, and as warning prickles at the back of my neck, his security arrives, standing behind me silently.

"Let's do that somewhere quieter, shall we?" he suggests, his easy smile belying the instruction in his tone.

Security follow us closely as Thomas guides me away from the rest of the attendees, the safety in numbers completely gone, and my fellow Angels nowhere to be seen.

"Shouldn't I have let the other Angels know I was leaving?" I ponder, looking back over my shoulder, hoping to catch someone's eye. Anyone could be a saviour at this point. "I wouldn't want to worry them unnecessarily." Especially when the Devils are already missing.

"We'll be catching up with them shortly, don't worry."

He holds another door open, waiting before I step inside to whisper instructions to his security. The library we find ourselves in is unexpected to say the least. There is tome after tome lined up meticulously as I look from one shelf to the next, avoiding the drinks laid out and the comfortable seating awaiting.

Thomas, however, does no such thing as he strides across the room to pour us both a drink, sipping the dark liquid in his glass whilst watching me intently.

"So, Ivy, why don't we sit?"

My feet are killing me, but the swirl of nervous energy

building in the pit of my stomach won't allow me to sit and be still and patient even if I wanted to, which I don't.

"As you wish." He shrugs as he makes himself comfortable in one of the large wingback chairs. "Your friends will be along shortly, but there's something I'd like to know if you don't mind?"

He waits for my acceptance and undivided attention as I return the beautiful, cloth-bound edition to its place before turning and nodding.

"If you could save one of them, only one, who would it be?"

Blood rushes in my ears. Is this a threat? A warning? Are they done and has one of them has failed? Is this an opportunity to save him if I can only pick the right one?

"That's an interesting question," I consider, stalling for time and wishing I still had that book in my hand so I could do something other than watch Thomas dissect my every movement.

"Take your time," he says. "I was expecting it to be tricky when I thought it was just two of them, but four? That's going to take a minute."

No shit.

I spent week after week going back and forth once before, never realising that I could have everything I wanted, and now he wants me to choose… again.

"Who did you think I was wrapped up with?" I ask, breaking his gaze and moving around the room, unable to stand still any longer.

"Nicholas Barrett and Wyatt Chambers."

"You were under the impression that Jacob and Leo

are together, then?" I ask, my heels clicking along the solid wood flooring.

"Yes."

For someone who knows so much, he's missed something pretty fucking important right there.

"I couldn't pick one of them," I admit, refusing to make eye contact. It's not a lie, but there's vulnerability in the truth I don't need him to see.

"Not even if their lives depended on it?" he asks ominously.

"Does it?" I ask, steeling my spine and looking up to catch the gaze that's already trained on me.

I throw the question out there before I have time to overthink it, the silence weighted with words unsaid as he tilts his head, examining every look, touch, and movement.

"Of course not," he eventually says, the smile on his face practiced and not in the slightest bit genuine, even around the mask. "I just thought it would be interesting conversation while we waited."

I nod, making my way to the tray of drinks and selecting one before joining him on the chairs, attempting to work out in my head how best to attempt to explain this to him.

"Do you love your wife?"

"Of course," he replies without thought.

"And if you had to choose only one part of her to keep, which would it be? She has two arms, two legs. If you could save only one, which would you choose?"

I sip the crisp champagne, knowing this is the only way he'll understand. They aren't four people I could ever choose from. They're one whole for me. There is no *which one would I save*, because that would be akin to removing a leg or an arm; they're each a part of the whole.

"That's an interesting comparison, but I'm not sure it's quite the same."

"How so?"

"My wife is more than the sum of her limbs. It's her heart, her soul, and her mind that connect with mine. Who does your soul connect with? Who does your heart long for? That's not an arm or a leg, it's something deeper."

"It is, and perhaps you'll never understand, but they're not just legs and arms on a partner. They're parts of me, too."

"So, which one of *my* limbs could I live without?" he asks, turning to top up his glass as he ponders his reply.

"Or which part of your heart, your soul? The part that brings you joy, the part that soothes your jagged edges? What about your protective instincts or your desire? Maybe you could live without knowing you're seen and heard, understood, but I couldn't."

He nods. "Very interesting."

Before he gets the opportunity to dissect our relationship any further, someone knocks on the door, waiting for a reply before Aimee and a very drunk Charlotte stumble through the doorway, confusion flickering over Aimee's face until a relief that really shouldn't be there, considering the circumstances, takes over. *Doesn't she realise this is more dangerous than we thought?*

"Ah, ladies. So kind of you to join us. Why don't you help yourself to a drink and come sit," Thomas offers. "I believe Penelope will be along momentarily and then we can begin."

"Begin what?" Aimee asks, stealing the thought straight from my head as she perches on the edge of the sofa, while Charlotte slumps with a glass in her hand.

"All in due course." He smiles, filling the quiet with inane questions about their evening as we wait, despite everything in me screaming that this is a dangerous mistake.

Two knocks interrupt us again, then Penelope arrives with a smile that's much more aware than Charlotte as she looks from me to Aimee and then to Thomas.

"Sorry to keep you waiting," she apologises. "Will Stephanie be along soon?"

"No, I've got all the Angels I need right here." Thomas smiles, a dimple popping in one cheek, and I can see Penelope's walls begin to weaken right in front of my eyes. "Darling, I think we're ready!" he calls.

My confusion must be evident, as is that of Aimee and Penelope as we look at each other, waiting for something to happen. Just when I think he's actually lost it and we're trapped in here with a crazy person, a side door opens, and his wife strides into the room with a silver tray in her hand—a juxtaposition to the dark green of her gown.

If she's been close enough to hear him call her, then there's no chance she's not heard our entire conversation. Her steely gaze flicks to mine briefly before she places the tray on the table beside her husband, smiling, then taking the seat the other side of him.

"So, ladies, as I'm sure you're aware, there's a little more to this evening than just bringing in the New Year." *Clearly.* "And as the Angels of Pendleton Prep, you've been afforded certain luxuries and leniencies that the Devils haven't," Thomas says.

"Tonight, we will be ringing the New Year in with a full set of initiates," his wife says with a smile, her eyes bright and excited.

"I thought you had all the Devils already?" I ask, my confusion clear.

"Oh, we do," she replies, her gaze flicking to mine.

"As I'm sure you're all aware, the Devils have been undertaking a series of challenges," Thomas says as Aimee stiffens beside me. "What you won't be aware of is the oath they took before they could begin this initiation."

"And now it's your turn," his wife finishes gleefully.

"And why doesn't Stephanie need to make this declaration?" Penelope asks, folding her hands together in her lap. "She's an Angel, too."

Unless Oliver is out, and she's already gone.

I hate that the thought flickers in my mind, as well as the combination of hope and disgust it triggers, but I have no control over it.

"Her Devil already took his oath, and she's tied to him now. Their fates are mirrored," the wife explains, standing and smoothing down the front of her dress. "We will all start this New Year together, linked through blood." She moves to the tray, lining up four small vials before picking up a long, silver knife.

"Fuck that," Charlotte slurs. "I'm not letting you slice me open with that thing. You must be insane. You're the people who broke George's leg, who made him disappear without a trace. I don't want linking to or tying to that kind of energy."

"Charlotte," Aimee says, turning and reaching out for her hand.

"No, Aims," Charlotte counters, shrugging her off. "You do what you want, but I'm not here for this."

"You're free to leave whenever it suits," Thomas says far too casually for it to be so simple. "But there are consequences to that."

"Ooh, you're going to make me disappear, too," she goads, waving her fingers in the air.

How much has she drunk… or snorted?

Sure, she's been upset about George, Tamsin, and everything else that's happened over the last few months, but she was excited about tonight—about the positive new start to the year. Where the hell did all that go?

"Ryke, can we get your help in here, please?" Thomas calls over his shoulder.

The door his wife entered through opens and closes before a man-mountain that must be part of their security enters quietly.

"This young lady has decided she no longer wishes to participate. Would you please show her on her way?" He gestures to Charlotte as she finishes her glass and hands it to Aimee, practically abandoning it in her lap.

"Come on, Charlotte. You can't really be willing to walk out now," Aimee pleads. "After everything we've done and been through. What about Harriet? Your Little Sister will miss you."

"I'm sure you'll work it out." Charlotte hiccups, smoothing down her dress. "Good fucking luck, girls.

You're going to need it."

I don't know why, but there's a tingling at the back of my neck. A warning. Thomas and his wife are way too casual about this. If there was a way for us to walk out of this in one piece we'd have known about it a long time ago. We certainly wouldn't have been presented to the secret society like trophy wives in the making.

Charlotte wobbles on her heels, her pupils blown as she fluffs out her dress and sets off towards the open door and the freedom beyond. She almost makes it too. The security guy Ryke steps forward, seemingly giving her space as he gestures her through, only time seems to slow down, everything happening faster than I thought possible.

He steps in, crowding her back as his arm comes up and across her body, the flash of silver glinting even in the dimmed lighting of the room before he quickly steps back, avoiding the spray of blood that gushes forth as he slits her throat quietly, without any ceremony.

"*Noooo!*" Aimee yells, dropping the glasses on the floor. Instantly, they shatter, glittering pieces of pain she forgets about as she rushes over while her friend slumps and falls as if in slow motion before our very eyes.

My heartbeat thunders in my ears as I sit in the chair, watching it all unfold, and unable to do anything about it. My stomach sinks as I watch Ryke pick Aimee up before she makes it to Charlotte, and I almost think we're about to lose another friend—watch someone else we care about be eliminated with nothing more than a discarded word and a swipe of his arm. But he just holds Aimee, not batting an eyelid as she throws herself around, hitting him and yelling, but the deed is done, the reminder set. There's no way out of this alive.

Penelope and I sit there dumbfounded, mouths open as the blood pools around Charlotte, seeping into the fabric of the rug beneath her as the reality of the situation hits us like a tonne of bricks. No matter what we thought about the situation we were in before, we know categorically now that there's no going back.

The seconds tick by, turning to minutes as Aimee's anger subsides, quickly replaced by devastating sobs. Surprisingly, Ryke holds her comfortingly until she stills before placing her on a chair at the side rather than back in the broken glass before collecting the discarded body of our friend and disappearing.

"It's just a pin prick," Thomas's wife says, pressing the top of the blade to the pad of her finger and watching the blood pool. "Nothing to be afraid of."

TWO

Leo

usic plays and people dance, the excitement of the New Year's Ball swirling around us like a vortex. It sucks everyone in and allows The Sect to play their games with us uninterrupted. But the more I look, the less I see, and panic begins to set in.

"They're not here, are they?" I ask, a lump forming in my throat as reality twists like a noose around my neck ever tighter.

Wyatt whispered, "Don't worry, they've got this," and then Oliver waltzed through the door, and not long after that, Nick did too. No Jacob. And now Ivy's nowhere to be found. What the hell kind of a joke is tonight to these people?

"I need a fucking smoke," I grumble under my breath, more than ready to get out of here and get some space, some clarity… some*thing*.

And it's amazing how the need for something I do so infrequently these days is clawing at my insides thanks to the stress. Maybe it's muscle memory, reaching for a smoke when shit gets tense, I don't know, but I itch for it, my skin practically vibrating.

"Let's get some air," Wyatt says with a nod before gesturing to Nick.

If the crumpled look of despondency on Nick's face is anything to go by, whatever thoughts are currently cascading around *his* brain can't be good. Well, he looks like he just found out his brother is probably dead, and his girlfriend is now missing.

Fuck. He's not dead. He can't be.

"I don't know about you, but as I don't usually smoke, I didn't bring any with me," I say, the words dripping with sarcasm as I push that dreadful thought to one side. "And where the hell would we even go?"

I haven't seen a single door or exit that isn't guarded tonight. There's no just 'walking out' happening here.

"It is terrible for your health," Wyatt says, shoving a barely-with-it Nick towards the side of the room, skirting around the dance floor as unobtrusively as he can manage while I follow.

He pushes through the dining room and an antechamber, plucking a couple of cigars from an open box on the desk before pressing on again and arriving in what looks to be a drawing room. A very *occupied* drawing room.

"Good evening," I say, plastering a smile on my face and nodding at one or two of the masked men while Wyatt continues to keep Nick moving, hoping we aren't drawing much attention to ourselves as I spot where he's heading.

The crisp evening air billows through the heavy drapes, and when I push through, I realise it's more than just a window, they are doors, and they're open.

"I found this earlier on," Wyatt says quietly as he steps out. "Didn't think it would be needed, but here we are."

Looking back over my shoulder, I take in the two dozen

or more male members of The Sect. There's not a skirt, dress, or ruffle in sight as they watch us closely. Wyatt and I may have been able to bluff our way through here—fake it until you make it and all that—but Nick can't fake shit right now.

Smiling, I push through the curtains, doing my best to pull them closed behind me before stepping away from the doorway and shoving Nick up against the wall, hoping he doesn't slide to the ground in a crumpled, pathetic heap if I let go.

"You're going to get yourself killed," I whisper-yell, getting in his face, because he can't do this. Not here. Not now. He can't crumple.

We're being watched, and any sign of weakness is going to be something they use against us.

"Have you got any matches?" Wyatt asks, seemingly oblivious to what's going on with Nick right now.

Peeking over my shoulder, I see Wyatt's unwrapping two cigars without a care in the world. Grabbing the zippo that always lives in my pocket, I hand it over, making sure Nick's got his weight on his feet before letting him go. The last thing we need is to actually have to carry this fucker back in there.

"I didn't know you smoked," I say, accepting the proffered cigar whilst keeping an eye on Nick in my periphery.

"Back at you," he comments before teaming a plume of smoke up to the heavens. "I like a cigar at special occasions. New Year, for example. There are a couple of good ones in my bag for when we all get back tonight."

The bitter smoke curls through my lungs. *One of us isn't coming back tonight.*

"I spoke with Jacob before we left," Wyatt says quietly, stepping in closer. "He's okay. He's going to be just fine."

"What?"

You can't come out with something like that and not follow it up with actual details.

He looks over his shoulder again, eventually deciding the coast is clear before whispering, "I got some info on my way home. He's okay for now, and it buys us some time." He pulls his phone out and opens up an app. "And it looks like Ivy is somewhere in the building, so she's probably fine, too."

So, he knew this was going to happen? He knew Jacob wouldn't make it? He couldn't have done. Except they gave me a choice at the end… maybe we all got one.

"Words, Wyatt," Nick growls out, no longer leaning despondently against the stone. "You're going to need to use more of your words than that."

I'm so engrossed in the insinuation that Jacob was okay that I almost forgot about the man to my side, the one barely holding it together. The man who was almost ready to throw it all in thinking he'd lost the two people who mean the world to him.

Sure, the five of us are a thing now, a unit, but both Jacob and Ivy are different. To Nick, anyway.

"I got a call earlier on. It was some contact of my father who had information about this evening," Wyatt continues, checking over his shoulder again before pulling the poison through the cigar, tasting and revelling in it, then releasing it into the night air while the two of us wait with bated breath.

"He said there'd be a challenge, that there's the option to walk away, and that should one fail, the opportunity would be presented for servitude or death."

"Servitude?"

"That the New Year would be brought in with *all* members," he continues without answering. "Even the Angels."

"So, they're in a challenge, too?"

"I don't know any more than you do, but I already had the necklace and bracelets designed and with me. I didn't want us to have to use them, but it helps to know we could find her if we needed to. I gave one of the bracelets to Jacob before we left, just in case."

"Necklace? Bracelet?" I ask, not following.

"There's a tracker in the necklace I gave to Ivy earlier on, and it's still showing here," Wyatt explains. "I can't pinpoint exactly where she is, but she's alive, and she's here. If they move, we'll know."

The necklace! Of course! And it was around the same time he asked Jacob to join him. Yeah, I thought they were up to *something else*, I sure as hell would have been, but it makes sense. The shower would cover any conversations they didn't want overheard.

"So, Jacob's alive?" Nick clarifies, his yearning tangible as he steps closer. "And Ivy's here somewhere too? They're not… they're not gone?"

"Well, they're both alive," Wyatt hedges, sounding much less confident than he did a moment ago. "And I don't have any more of a plan than this, but it's a start."

Nick lets out a shuddering breath, closing his eyes as he drops his head back against the cool stone. "I think I know who to ask for help. The Sect told me tonight."

"Huh? Actually, never mind. Why didn't you mention this before?" I ask, dropping whatever thoughts Nick has in favour of the details Wyatt hasn't shared.

It sounds like his father knew this was coming. Mine, too, if the 'new revelations' comment was anything to go by. Oh, and Dex and Blaise, as well. Well, Blaise at the very least. Fuck, this is getting complicated.

I will never in my life forget the way my heart sank when Nick walked through the doorway. It wasn't disappointment. At least not only that, because I do want him to make it through. And if anyone is going to be able to find their way out of servitude, it's going to be Jacob. Let's be honest, Nick would have opened his mouth within the first five minutes, and they'd be taking back the offer, but I really wanted him to pull through this.

Maybe what he found out was too much, too awful. Or maybe the video from his father tipped him over the edge. Maybe it really was out of his hands, but Nick kicking off here, now, in the middle of a members-only event, isn't going to get Jacob back or help us to find Ivy.

Sure, I understand the anger Nick wore as armour, just briefly. The need, the desperation, but Wyatt had already whispered it was under control, and knowing just how under the microscope we are tonight, I couldn't pry any further, but I held onto that tiny glimmer of hope. Held onto it tightly.

"There wasn't any time—no opportunity," Wyatt

replies, watching my smoke as it makes its way into the night before I throw it on the ground and stamp it out.

"That tastes like shit."

"That tastes like the expensive cigars you enjoy over a sweet brandy with friends," Wyatt counters. "But I suppose this isn't that moment."

"No."

"It did the job," Nick comments, the life coming back into him now. "Wyatt got to fill us in, and you don't look like you're about to murder someone."

"Yeah, well, looks can be deceiving," I grumble. "But you don't look like you're about to curl up into a ball and hide, now, so that's good."

"Fuck you."

"In your dreams."

Just because he looks like Jacob doesn't mean he's actually anything like him at all, and the deeper I get to know them both, the more obvious it becomes, to me at least. He's practically ready to square up, that anger finally finding a safe way to release, only we're currently in the middle of an event, in suits, not the sparring ring. And is that straw on his jacket?

"So, let me just get this straight," Nick says, breaking eye contact with me and looking straight at Wyatt, his anger beginning to spill over. "You knew something was going to happen tonight with us and the Angels, and you knew we could choose to serve The Sect until the rest of us figured this shit out, and you didn't say anything?"

"They're only bringing the Angels into the fold, from what I can gather. They're not at any risk, and there's no way in hell either of you two were going to be thrown by the deep, dark secrets that were going to be sent your way tonight. I did what needed to be done." Wyatt shrugs, bringing what's left of the cigar to his lips.

Someone steps out of the open door, and I shove Nick in the shoulder, catching his attention before he says something to land us all in the shit.

"Gentlemen, I believe we're needed in the ballroom," a man in a dark blue mask says. I think he's one who greeted us when we first arrived tonight.

"That's a shame," Wyatt says, looking longingly at the remaining cigar before putting it out.

Nick barges past him, anger first, as he heads for the door, leaving me to follow. *What the hell is he going to do now?*

"I swear if there is so much as one hair on Ivy's head out of place, I'm going to break his face," he mumbles under his breath, the room luckily empty as I catch up.

"She's not stupid," I say, falling in step. "I'm sure she came prepared."

And this is why I gave her the thigh strap for the knife.

Stopping dead, he pins me with an unimpressed look, clearly thinking the exact same thing as me while we wait for Wyatt and the guy in the blue mask to catch up before continuing on, his anger simmering away, barely restrained.

Anger has got to be better than the pathetic devastation that was seeping from his every pore five minutes ago, but, this?

Nick stomps ahead as the three of us follow in his wake. I understand the sentiment, but this really isn't the place or the time for that. After all, if we thought everything was 'seen and heard' inside the house, it's got to be even worse here.

In his haste, we take a wrong turn, ending up back in the entranceway rather than the ballroom, much to his displeasure, until we catch the sound of animated conversation coming from somewhere nearby. Soon there's a couple appearing, with the Angels following subduedly.

I'm not the only one who notices them, and Nick rushes straight towards Ivy, but both Stephanie and Charlotte are missing. Surely, they've not lost people tonight as well, have they? Wyatt said all they were doing was bringing everyone into the fold.

Wyatt and I hold back, unease creeping down my spine as our masked hosts talk quietly.

"I trust you're capable of making your way in?" the gentleman that walked with us asks, gesturing to the heavy wooden doors just a few steps away. "I believe we're needed."

"Of course," Wyatt replies, while I nod.

Wyatt steps closer to Ivy, offering his arm to her. She rests one hand on Wyatt's and one on Nick's. I follow behind silently. Penelope and Aimee barely look up, and none of them are speaking. Something is very wrong here, yet they all look perfectly fine. There's not a cut, graze, bruise, or limp amongst them and, other than two of them being missing, I can't for the life of me work it out. Wyatt said they were all being brought into the fold, so they can't be far away, can they? Except that Ivy's not so much as realised Jacob isn't even here. That's not right.

The six of us head into the ballroom, the heat and the noise stifling after the silence of the evening air outside. Two ladies watch us with interest from the bar. Once we arrive around the edge of the dance floor, it's clear we're just in time.

"Where the hell did you lot go?" Oliver asks, nudging my shoulder as he tucks Stephanie under his arm

"For a smoke."

"And you found the rest of them. Nice work." He nods. "Although, it sounds like they ditched Steph. Not very friendly if you ask me."

"I don't think it quite happened that way," I hedge, aware that's probably what the Angels thought when they realised we were gone, too.

"Well, whatever. You're here now."

Yeah, but where are Jacob and Charlotte?

"Ladies and gentlemen!" echoes around the room, the music going quiet in its wake. "Thank you for joining us this evening. It's always an honour to spend time with you all."

A ripple of replies flurry across the room, a glass or two being raised in agreement as a waitress appears with a tray of champagne flutes. I can't see the man up front for all the people between here and there, but I can hear the arrogance in his tone and instantly, I know I'm not going to like whatever else he has to say.

"If you could all take a glass and raise it together. To the new blood. May their New Year's revelations help them on the paths they forge this year."

"To the new blood!" reverberates back, with glasses

being raised, and looks being sent our way.

"To the active members of The Sect. May our days be quiet, our pockets full, and our beds always lively."

Gross.

"To the members!" booms around the room, another drink being taken as we awkwardly join in.

"Sounds like a promising future," Oliver whispers with a wink.

"And finally, to those we've lost along the way. May they rest in peace."

A lump forms in my throat, and it takes way more than I anticipated to push it down. I know he's alive and safe… for now. But that statement, for all intents and purposes, could have been about Jacob. I don't drink, couldn't even if I tried, and Ivy's sniffle has my hackles raised and on high alert. Where the hell is Charlotte?

We got rushed in here last minute, and then they went into the toasts so quickly that we barely had time to say hello. I assumed wherever she was, Stephanie was with her, and yet here Stephanie stands with her man, but Charlotte is nowhere in sight.

"Have you seen Charlotte?" I ask, leaning to Oliver.

"Nah, man, I just found Stephanie chatting with some women when I came in. Apparently, everyone else disappeared about half an hour ago. Didn't even bother to let her know they were fucking off."

Everyone…

"Great, thanks," I grumble.

"Have you got your head on properly now?" he asks. "You know there are only three that go through at the end of this. It would be good if you were on my side," he whispers before looking at Nick and Wyatt.

"There aren't any sides in this, and nobody wins but them," I reply hoarsely, knowing he's going to be the one failing next time.

There's no way The Sect would stack the deck in favour of a man of his stature—not against three bloodline members. It's sad, but whatever they decide to throw at us next is not going to play to his strength.

"Happy New Year, folks. Enjoy the rest of your evening!" the voice calls, and apparently I've missed the countdown as the bell chimes, a year beginning anew, without Jacob.

I don't know why it hurts so much. This time last year, I didn't even know who he was, only the reputation of the man who was supposed to be my competition, but somewhere along the road he buried under my skin. They all have.

The music recommences, and Oliver and Stephanie move away, which is probably for the best. Some small tables have been set up, a few of the older members taking the opportunity to rest as they watch everyone dancing and enjoying themselves.

Someone knocks into me before the doors beside us fling open to reveal a dining room transformed to allow guests to sit, talk, and take refuge from the noise whilst still being involved in the festivities.

"The cars will be here in thirty minutes," one of the waiters explains with a nod before he disappears again.

"Well, I guess that's more time than Cinderella got," I say, attempting to break the awkward silence as we all move into the new space. "Nobody's hiding a glass slipper under their skirts, are they?"

The joke falls flat as Aimee slumps onto one of the sofas with a sigh, the weight of the world seemingly still on her shoulders.

Nick twirls Ivy, her skirt blowing out around her as they whisper quietly, and Wyatt comes to my side, clearly picking up on the same thing I have. There's more to this than just tying them into The Sect, but we're not alone, and we can't exactly start quizzing them here.

I'm still not sure how to form the words to explain that Jacob's gone… failed… alive but no longer with us. Well, for now, at least.

Nick keeps Ivy moving, the two of them whispering as I take a seat on the sofa next to Aimee. Penelope sits beside her, quietly holding her hand.

"What happened?"

"I don't know," Aimee admits, staring blankly at the floor. "One minute we were talking, and the next…" she trails off.

"The next?"

"There was a nice man," Penelope picks up. "We were dancing, laughing, and then he says we should get a drink. " She scoffs out a dark laugh, and I stiffen.

"Okay, then what happened?" Wyatt asks soothingly as he drops to the floor in front of them, reaching for their clasped hands.

"He took us somewhere else out there, and he didn't stay, but the girls were there," she says, her thoughts still far off.

"Okay. All the girls?" I clarify.

"Not Stephanie, because she's linked to Oliver, so she didn't have to swear allegiance to The Sect," she replies, but Aimee is still lost in her head.

So, it was just oaths, after all. The relief on my face must be obvious as Wyatt's gaze flicks to mine, but it's not over yet.

"Penelope, where's Charlotte?" he asks.

"No, don't," Aimee pleads, suddenly bursting forth before our eyes. "Don't say it. I can't…"

"She didn't want to take the oath," Penelope continues, undeterred. "She said it was stupid."

Our concerned gazes fly to Penelope and the way her hands tremble beneath Wyatt's. If she didn't take the oath, and she isn't here now, then maybe she's where Jacob is. Maybe she's okay.

"But you guys did?" Wyatt asks, turning their hands over and looking for a mark. "You two and Ivy."

Aimee nods, barely holding back tears as she holds up her finger to reveal a tiny cut in the pad, and that's when I notice it: a smudge of red at the bottom of her dress.

Charlotte's not with Jacob. She's dead, and that's why the three of them look fucking traumatised, because they are.

Whatever happened, they were there. They were witness to it, and now they're tied into The Sect, too. There's no way Ivy's going to leave here without Jacob, or knowing about Jacob, on the back of this. Fuck.

"We need to get out of here," I whisper, looking around.

We've been dragged out, shown off, and put through the

wringer. All of us. And now, barely moments into the New Year celebrations, we're being sent away again. This wasn't about starting the new year with insight and revelations. It was about tying up loose ends.

"She's gone," I whisper with a shake of my head. Neither of the girls are capable of saying it out loud. "She's gone, and she's not coming back."

Aimee holds back a sob as her shoulders shake, doing her best to keep it together as I take a furtive glance around the room.

We're being observed.

It's not obvious. No tittering women or glowering men keeping an eye on us, but it's a feeling at the base of my skull. An awareness that pulls around me. They're watching to see what we do, to see how we react to losing not one, not a couple, but *two* individuals.

Two individuals tied to us so tightly, I'm not sure how we'll ever recover.

"We don't have long before the carriage turns back into a pumpkin," Wyatt says, carrying on my line of thought from before as he squeezes Penelope's hands and calls to Nick. "You'd better make sure Cinderella has both those slippers on."

Nick looks confused as Ivy shudders in his hold, the two of them finally coming to join us.

"We've been lucky that the horses didn't turn back into mice at midnight, and nobody's gown is falling to tatters yet, but our time here is almost done," Wyatt continues.

There'll be time to fall apart soon. At home, safely in the confines of the rooms that are still being watched and listened to, just more subtly than this.

"Shall we take one last spin around the dance floor and show these people that we're stronger than they think we are?" Wyatt whispers, doing his best to pull Aimee and Penelope out of the sadness that's wrapping around them.

"I can't," Aimee says, staring far, far away. "I can't stop seeing it."

"And I can't dance to this," I admit quietly. "Not all of us were brought up with silver spoons."

The words are bitter on my tongue.

It's not their money that's afforded them this complacency. No, we've all got that. It's their lifestyles, their class, or my father's lack of it. Wrap that up with a bundle of shame and the shambles that this evening has been and I'm feeling flat and defeated. Almost as much of a mess as Aimee looks right now.

"Why don't you guys stay?" Ivy says, her hand coming to my shoulder. "Come on, Penelope. We'll show them."

Penelope hovers, acquiescing when Aimee eventually shoos her away, taking my hand instead of Wyatt's as I pull her into my side, watching the four of them disappear back into the ballroom.

"What about Nick?" she asks quietly.

"He's with Ivy."

"Oh." She dabs beneath her eyes with a tissue. "I thought that was…" Her sentence trails off, and I suddenly realise she'd got them confused; mistaken Nick's care and consideration for Jacob's. "So, where's Jacob?"

My heart squeezes in my chest, and I close my eyes, willing the pain away before admitting. "I don't know."

THREE

Ivy

The car is silent as we make our way down the driveway and back to the house, the new year not nearly as fortuitous as we might have hoped. Stephanie and Oliver are nowhere to be seen, but a line seems to have been drawn between the couple and the rest of us over the last few weeks. Perks of mirroring your fate, I suppose.

The guys are waiting for us on the doorstep when we pull up, but they don't wait for the driver to get out, instead sweeping down the stairs and opening the doors as they help us and our huge dresses out and back into the safety of the house without any ceremony. The door closes with a finality that has a lump forming in my throat.

"I'd say thank you for a lovely night, but, uh…" Penelope says as she releases Nick's arm, stepping out of her heels.

"Yeah," Nick replies.

"Does anyone want a night cap?" Wyatt asks, gesturing to the kitchen as he pulls his jacket off and drapes it over his arm.

"I just don't understand why she would do that," Aimee

says tearfully. "Why would she *do* that?"

"I don't know, honey." Penelope wraps an arm over her shoulder and guides her up the stairs. "Why don't you stay with me tonight? There's no point us both being alone."

Aimee sniffles but nods as Nick, Wyatt, Leo and I loiter in the entranceway, the Christmas lights twinkling on the tree behind us cheerily.

When I lost Tamsin, we hid. When I thought we'd lost Nick, we drank. But neither of those options seem fitting right now.

Tonight, I saw my friend murdered—a sneak peek of what might have happened to Tamsin, and whilst Jacob is safe, he's still not here. There's a gap, a hole, and as I look around, I'm not the only one that's feeling it. Nobody makes any hints about going up to bed, despite the early hour of the morning, and it's not like we have to be anywhere else today or tomorrow. We have a few days now before classes begin.

Nick stares vacantly across the room, looking at everything and seeing nothing, a pain that none of us are going to understand held in his unfocused gaze.

Taking Nick's hand, I move us through to the den, pushing him down into one of the sofas before helping to take off his jacket and shoes. Wyatt finds something on the TV, and Leo appears with beers as we all get comfortable, holed up with nothing more than the soft, white light from the tree and whatever's playing quietly to keep us company.

Nobody says anything, but I take both Nick and Leo's hands in mine as we let the events of the evening settle in our bones.

"Have you been smoking?" I ask, looking between the

three of them, the murky smell permeating the air.

"Cigars." Wyatt nods.

"It fucking stinks."

"Sorry, angel," Leo says quietly. "It's been a bit of a night."

Understatement of the year.

"I have some good ones somewhere... to celebrate the new year," Wyatt says as he tips the bottle back, taking a swig of the cold beer, his Adam's apple bobbing. "Let's save them for a better moment, though."

I nod, shuffling down and resting my head on Nick's shoulder, my skirt making it awkward as more than one of the jewels dig into places I wish they didn't. We're here together, but nobody is quite ready for the night to end. So, we have a drink, watch something on the TV, and do our best to hold it together, only to be woken what feels like nothing more than a few hours later.

"Don't you lot have a perfectly good room upstairs?" Oliver asks as Nick's shoulder moves beneath my head, rousing me.

"Huh?" I grumble, attempting to sit up and rub the sleep from my eyes.

"I'm hitting the gym if any of you want to shake off whatever the hell this is," Oliver says, shaking his hand in our general direction and turning away before I'm even fully aware of what's going on around me.

Nick stretches his arms over his head, cracking his neck from side to side before pulling me into his embrace and burying his nose in my hair. He probably crosses paths with a pin or two if the strange noise that comes from him is anything to go by.

The TV still plays in the corner of the room, and when Wyatt pushes back the curtains, letting the grey winter morning in, I wouldn't have been surprised to find it still the middle of the night, but it's not.

"Good morning, chick," Wyatt says, placing a kiss on my cheek.

"Morning."

"I guess we fell asleep," Nick comments, looking around the den.

Half a dozen empty bottles are piled up on the coffee table. There's a blanket abandoned on the floor along with my heels, some jackets, shoes, and a rogue waistcoat.

"Can I just say that last year, I did not wake up alone, sober, or with a crick in my neck," Leo says, coming through the doorway with a fistful of mugs in one hand and a carafe of coffee in the other.

"I guess it can only go up from here, then, huh?" Wyatt asks.

"Let's not jinx that," I call after him as he heads out, hopefully on the way for sugar and cream. "You're amazing," I say, the rich aroma filling the room as Leo pours the coffee. "Hang on, did you change already?"

Long gone is the charcoal suit he wore last night, the shirt now replaced with a basic white tee and shorts, along with a towel thrown around his neck.

"Yeah, my cardio is all done. I figured the coffee would be ready for pouring by now, but I wasn't expecting Oliver to be up and moving yet. I guess he'll keep me company in the ring for half an hour or so."

He drinks the coffee in one go, red-hot and black, before Wyatt even makes it back.

"I might come down in a bit. Getting my arse moving should probably be higher on the priority list than it has been," I admit, thinking of how many things I've let slide since coming here.

"No rush." He winks, the small smile not reaching his eyes as he walks out.

Wyatt crosses his path, confusion flashing over his features. "Something I said?" he asks, watching Leo's retreating form.

"Nah. He's going to kick Oliver's arse again," Nick explains.

After dropping the empty bottles in the bin, Wyatt shuffles the coffee table closer as he makes our coffees, the three of us huddled around it quietly. I turn the TV off, finding the remote hidden in one of the folds of my skirt as I do my best to pull myself out of the sofa.

A jacket falls off the arm, crumpling to the floor as I get a flashback to last night. Charlotte's dark hair pooling in the thick crimson seeping into the carpet that she'd been stood on just moments before. I blink and it's gone. Instead, I'm looking at another discarded piece of clothing, but the damage is done as my stomach twists and turns.

"You okay?" Wyatt asks, his concern clear.

"Yeah. No. Fuck! Last night really happened," I admit.

Wyatt nods, catching my gaze and gesturing to Nick.

My eyes widen as it all finally sinks in. The reason we didn't want to go up in the first place. Why Leo looks like he's barely slept and is about ready to murder someone.

Jacob's not here.

But he's safe… for now.

"What time is it?" Nick asks, pulling his phone out.

"Half nine," Wyatt replies.

"They might still be here," Nick muses, scrolling through his contacts. "Give me two."

He picks up his coffee, slides his shoes on his feet, and walks out, the front door closing behind him with a thud.

"Shall we take these upstairs?" Wyatt asks, sipping his coffee. "Or do you need five minutes?"

"Let's wait for Nick and go up together. We may as well finish our coffees. There's no point carrying this lot up only to have to bring it all back down again."

He nods, sitting opposite me as he watches with interest. Of all of us, he's the least intimately involved with Jacob, but he barely seems affected. Not that I think he should be falling over crying and wailing—although a little emotion would be expected—but he's totally calm and collected, trusting the bracelet.

"So, what happens from here?" I ask.

"I don't know," he admits, kicking his ankle up over his knee as he leans back. "We've got another challenge coming up, and whatever that is going to be will no doubt be complicated. This is the last one, after all."

"More complicated than last night?"

Was that only last night? It feels like a lifetime ago, but also nothing more than a few seconds, but as the jewels on my dress catch my eye, it's more than real and happening right now.

"That was the semi-final, so to speak. I can only imagine

that whatever is yet to come will be bigger and 'better' than that."

"And Jacob?"

"Is safe, I'm sure. Let's just focus on one thing at once."

Because, of course, The Sect see everything, hear everything. Our thoughts, hopes, dreams, and anything we may be wanting to do about getting Jacob back with us can't be discussed here, not safely anyway.

By the time we've finished our coffees and cleared up, Nick has returned, and the three of us trudge upstairs, the mood in the house sombre, despite the festive cheer we've attempted to force into it. Whatever happened to autumn sunshine and parties around the pool? Now, the winter is here, and the darkness is wrapping tightly around us. So tight that we can't get out. Nobody can.

The first floor is silent, but there's music coming from Stephanie and Oliver's room as we pass. Taking a deep breath, I push open the door to our room, not in the slightest bit ready to begin life without one of the men I swore to love, protect, and care for.

The room looks exactly the same, only not, and where I ran from the pain of losing Tamsin into the arms of these guys, there's nowhere else to go now.

"He's always leaving his shit everywhere," Nick grumbles, picking up a rogue shirt and heading into the walk-in wardrobe, and I follow.

Angrily, he throws it into the washing basket along with his jacket while I carefully place my heels on the shelf— the empty shelf—my skirt rustling being the only sound. Nick's agitation brews as he yanks off his shirt, refusing to acknowledge the empty space where Jacob's clothes used to be, the shirt abandoned his rather than his brother's.

He barely sees the clothes he picks out and throws on the vanity. Wyatt is in the shower attempting to wash away the evening's events, but eventually, it all spills over. Nick's rage tangles up with the devastation as he throws his clothes from place to place, venting everything.

"Just… why?" Nick growls, dropping onto the bench and yanking fruitlessly at the laces on his shoes. "How did Wyatt know? Why did it have to be Jacob? How long are we supposed to carry on like this?"

Stepping behind him, I place my hands on his shoulders and close my eyes, waiting for all the thoughts tumbling out of his mouth to finish and for him to rest his head back against my stomach. It takes a minute, more than one, as all the thoughts that have been running rampant finally come to an end.

"It was going to be someone eventually, but there's no way he'll be left behind," I whisper. "Make your calls. Let Leo and Wyatt do the same. We'll find a way."

He takes a deep breath in, the air shuddering out when he releases it. His huge hands come up to cover mine as I look down into those never-ending, hazel depths.

"It's going to take some time. Lean on us."

I leant on them. I had no choice. Now, he needs do the same.

Nodding, he squeezes my hand before going back to getting changed. He unfastens my dress and helps me get out of all the layers, but there's nothing sexual crackling between us. Just two people holding each other up.

After throwing on some jeans and a tee, I'm working on getting all the pins out of my hair when Wyatt joins us, my phone in his hand.

"This thing was having some kind of shit fit," he says handing it over as the alarm starts blaring again.

"Fuck, I forgot all about that." I sigh, turning it off. "Peer training meeting."

"On New Year's Day?" Nick asks.

Nodding, I run a brush through my hair and gently massage a face wipe over my skin, rubbing angrily at the stubborn mascara that won't come off.

"Do you need anything doing or getting?" Nick asks, catching my gaze in the mirror.

Moving my hair to the side, he steps closer and unfastens the necklace, placing it carefully back in the box. The long-sleeved, white top hugs his biceps and shoulders as he moves. Something so normal, so everyday, but still sexy as hell.

"Just the TV thing, I think, if you wouldn't mind?" I ask.

"How long do we have?" he asks, staring longingly at the empty spaces where Jacob's clothing used to be.

Someone knocks on the door, and I realise the alarm must have been going for a while before Wyatt heard it. And as the voices carry through from the suite and into the walk-in, it's clear he's let the girls in, too.

"I guess that answers that question," I reply with a smile, looking at Nick. "Did you get what you needed on the phone earlier?"

"Yeah. Carlos and Tino are still in London. They're

gonna come and visit before they head back to Italy. I just need to check dates and stuff, then they'll let me know."

"I don't know who that is, but hopefully I get chance to meet them." I smile.

"Carlos is my sister's fiancé. We'll grab dinner or something," he replies distractedly. "I might go check on Leo once you're all set up."

"That sounds like a great idea. Maybe you should take Wyatt for back up."

Not that either of them would need the support, but if Leo and Oliver are hard at it in the ring, then two of them being available to pry them apart may be needed.

He squeezes my shoulder as I stand and head out to find the girls already getting comfortable and setting up, the meeting already in its holding screen on the huge TV. Stephanie and Penelope are deep in conversation while Aimee flicks through the pages of her notebook, clearly seeing none of it.

Quickly, I dash into the office and grab my stuff off the shelf as Nick and Wyatt wave and leave.

"I totally forgot about this," I admit, dropping into a bean bag beside Aimee. "Thank God for calendar reminders."

"Same," she says. "Both mine and Penelope's went off at the same time and scared us half to death."

Before we have chance to talk about anything else, the screen bursts into life, with Liselle appearing front and centre.

"Happy New Year, Angels," she sing-songs, her smile resplendent. "I hope you had an exciting time last night and are ready for all the things this year has to bring."

If last night was anything to go by, then definitely not.

"I'm going to let Amy take over with your usual training, but first, I wanted to let you know about your final exam, so-to-speak."

She makes no comment about the fact that Charlotte isn't here, or that we all look like we've just rolled out of bed and into the meeting. Instead, she's fresh-faced and ready to tackle the new year with something ridiculous, no doubt.

"Exam?" Stephanie asks with the tilt of her head. "I didn't realise this was something we were being tested on."

Because everything we've been doing so far has been for the good of our hearts and souls. Really?

"Well, yes and no," Liselle hedges. "The pièce de résistance of the Big Sister-Little Sister programme is its annual fundraising gala, and you fine ladies will be using all the skills and training you've acquired to turn it into the best event in years."

"This really is something we take great pride in, and the more money we raise, the more young women we can support and lend a helping hand to," Amy adds, appearing in the picture beside Liselle.

"Come up with a concept and a location. You'll get a budget and a basic guest list, but getting big investors in and making the most of the ones we provide is down to you," Liselle finishes.

"A location is going to be down to budget," Penelope comments, pen poised.

"You'll have a full brief in your email by the time you're finished here," Liselle replies. "Have fun."

We spend the next hour listening to Amy and taking notes, and by the time she's finally done, we have an email prepped and waiting, as promised.

"At least if we're organising it there won't be any surprises at this one," Penelope comments as she looks over the notes we've been given.

"That budget is not going to cover a decent venue, never mind catering and entertainment," Stephanie comments dismissively.

"So, we need to fundraise for the fundraiser. Great," Aimee grumbles.

"Well, we have a date, so that's a start. It could be further away… but I guess we'll just have to do our best to pull this off," I comment. "And if they've already warned the potential guest list to be available, then we're rolling before we begin."

"You sound like you know what you're doing," Aimee says, side-eying me.

"It's a giant dinner party. Easy." I shrug.

"So, we're doing a dinner, then? Not canapés and a band?" Stephanie asks, jumping ahead.

"We can do whatever," I reply. "It was just an explanation."

"How about we do a charity auction?" Penelope suggests, wrapping and unwrapping a lock of hair around her finger. "It says here that we've got to raise money individually, but then coordinate the event together. If we have to coordinate our own lots, that would be an easy way to work out who raised what."

"And we'd be able to use whoever or whatever we

wanted for that, would we? Because I have a lot of friends I could hit up in the sports world," Stephanie says confidently.

"It doesn't say specifically here that we *can't* do that, just that this is a student fundraiser, and so it must be tastefully appropriate," I reply, reading from the notes.

"I wasn't going to suggest a strip club," Aimee says with an unimpressed scoff as she closes her books. "But I guess it's good to have some boundaries, not that these people seem to pay much attention to them, anyway."

"Canapés would work for an auction style event, too, rather than a dinner," I ponder, attempting to keep us on track and not fall into the rabbit hole of the people missing here today: Charlotte and Jacob. "It would be cheaper, too, and this budge isn't huge. How many leads have they given us to start with?"

"Thirty-two," Penelope says, cringing. Yeah, that could be better. "I'm sure we all know half a dozen people who we could invite though. I would have said around sixty would be a good number, don't you think? Small enough to be an intimate gathering, but enough to build up some competition over the lots."

"If we're having a small gathering, we probably only need a dozen or so items. So, that's like, what? Three or four each? Easy." Stephanie grins, clearly feeling confident about this.

"Aimee, are you good with all that as a plan? If we each coordinate three or four items and half a dozen potential investors, we can catch up in a week or so to make sure we don't have a lot of cross over or duplications. Then we can work out a venue and invitations." I nod.

"Today is not the day I get excited about any of this. And right now, I honestly couldn't care less. So, if this is what you all want to do, then let's do it," Aimee replies with a defeated shrug of her shoulders. "Now, if you don't mind, I'm going to go and move my stuff out of that soulless room."

Quietly, she collects her things and leaves. The losses over the last few months are clearly stacking up on her shoulders.

"She's going to stay with me. Although it doesn't seem there's much safety in numbers, either," Penelope says as she makes a few notes.

"Well, this is going to be exciting," Stephanie interjects before I have time to reply. "Finally, we get to do something that shows off our skills."

Either she has no ability to read a room, or she just doesn't care. As Wyatt sticks his head around the door to check If we're finished, the three of us pack up and call it a day, agreeing to book some time in again soon.

"That looked tense," Wyatt comments once the door closes behind them. "Is everything okay?"

"Fine. I think we're all just coming to terms with what happened last night in our own ways, and Stephanie wasn't there when…" I swallow, thinking back to the flash of silver. "She wasn't there when it happened. So, she's got all the sympathy of a pea right now."

"I didn't realise peas had the ability to do that," he replies with a wink, his arm landing around my shoulders as he joins me on the sofa. "Tell me, if we weren't here, what would you usually be doing on New Year's Day?"

"Ooh, good question." My leg brushes up against his, electricity sparking between us as I turn. "Well, last year, Tamsin and I went out to a party with some big arse businessman. His younger brother had been chasing after my sexy best friend for months and not taking the hint that she wasn't interested, so this was going to be the ultimate fuck you. Except when we got there, he turned out to be engaged, and the raging party was actually a dinner with two dozen people and not nearly enough cocktails. Needless to say, we skipped out early and gate-crashed somewhere else."

"Sounds fun."

"It wasn't planned," I say, thinking of the mad dash we had attempting to get a car from one place to the other last minute. "But it was awesome. New Year's Day was spent recovering at my place because my parents were away for the weekend. We ate pizza in our pyjamas and spent the day doing absolutely nothing. What about you?"

"Family dinner with my parents is a thing. They like to have us all together so we can *start it off right*. Whatever that means." He rolls his eyes, lost to memories of New Year's Day at home. "Neither of those are much like today, though, are they?"

"Not really," I admit looking at the notebooks laid out. The work I've done and the morning the guys have spent in the gym isn't exactly relaxing or bonding. "But... there is time for us to pizza and chill this afternoon, and we'll be having a beautiful dinner with the rest of the house this evening as usual. So, it's not over yet. Where are Nick and Leo, anyway?"

"Still in the gym."

"What? It's been hours."

"I left them doing weights, so at least they're not kicking the shit out of each other anymore." He cringes, tucking a lock of hair behind my ear.

"Is Nick even up to that?"

I know it's been a while since his run in with The Sect, but broken bones take more than a month or so to heal properly.

"He's hurt, angry, and probably a whole ton of emotions that I wouldn't be able to name right now, but they both know their limits. Let them reach them before they have to face this room again, yeah?"

I nod in understanding.

I still haven't stepped foot in the pool house since losing Tamsin. I can't even begin to imagine how the two of them feel about coming back in here knowing that Jacob is gone.

"Maybe relaxing up here isn't the answer, but we could hole up in the movie room?" I offer.

"Sounds like a plan." He nods, his smile brightening the room. "Did you see the bracelet I got you?"

"No?"

"Okay, hang on."

He jumps up and heads into the walk-in wardrobe before coming out with a box much like the one he gave me last night.

"It's not quite the same as the necklace, but since you've got gifts from the others, I thought it would be nice if you had something a little more everyday that you could wear that would keep you safe," he explains, opening it up.

The delicate bracelet is beautiful, with diamonds and

obsidian beans alternating on a silver chain, and a little silver teardrop by the clasp.

"It's beautiful, thank you," I say as he pulls it out and fastens it around my wrist.

Then he shuffles the bracelets on his wrist, pulling out a simple strip of leather with a single clump of obsidian suspended between a series of complicated looking twists. "I know mine isn't quite the same, but Jacob has one, and hopefully Nick and Leo agree to wear theirs, too."

"That's so thoughtful. Even though he's not with us right now, he's still got a little part of us keeping him safe. That's beautiful."

"I fucking hope so," he admits.

FOUR

Nick

After checking the coffee pot is still hot for the sixth time, I adjust the cups on the table, straightening one out only to find it's wonkier than before, then moving it back.

"Will you chill the fuck out, man?" Leo says, leaning against the doorway. "I'm getting stressed out just watching you."

"Then, go find yourself somewhere else to be. I don't need you here for this."

Ivy will be here shortly, I hope. The two of us can get the help we need without his interference.

"Are you sure? You're twitchy as fuck." He smirks, and I'm more than ready to launch one of the cups at his face when the doorbell rings—three knocks echoing afterwards.

"Yes. I'm fine. Now, piss off," I hiss, passing him and heading through the entranceway as I straighten my shirt cuff again, hoping and praying he's gone by the time I turn around.

Plastering a smile on my face, I pull open the door in time for my sister to practically tumble through it as she wraps her arms around my middle and pulls me in for a hug.

"This is not what I pictured when you said university campus, Nicky," she says with a smile.

"It's a preparatory academy," I correct. "Not a university." She never listens.

"Either way, nice digs." She smiles, lighting up the room as Carlos and Tino follow her in quietly.

Tino nods at me before heading away. Now I know who they are and what they do, I realise he's no doubt checking the exits and security around the place.

No need to worry there, my friend, this place is loaded with security.

"Thanks for coming. I've got coffee prepared," I say, pushing that thought aside and shaking Carlos's hand.

"Hopefully it's better than whatever crap your mother keeps in," Carlos replies, the edge of his mouth kicking up into something akin to a smile.

The two of them look like something from a magazine as he folds Sophie's arm into his and walks through the entranceway. Carlos's dark hair is pushed back off his face, his thick, wool coat hanging from one arm. Sophie is all long legs and tanned skin in a dress that hugs each of the curves I really wish she didn't have. Italy suits her.

"Leo, this is my sister Sophie and her fiancé Carlos Mariotti. The man behind you is their friend Tino. Everyone, this is Leo. He's Jacob's partner, and he'll be leaving us to it any minute," I hint.

He doesn't take it, instead crossing his arms over his chest and leaning back against the frame as Tino pushes past.

"And where exactly is my favourite little brother?" Sophie asks, pain slicing through my chest.

"He's not here at the minute," I reply, really not able to explain that in here. I knew we should have done this somewhere else. "Let's talk about that at dinner. First, I want to know what's going on with you guys. How was Italy at Christmas?" I ask, joining her on the sofa as Carlos takes a wingback chair where he can see the door.

Yeah, his mafia ties are totally obvious now I know about them.

Over the next half an hour or so, we catch up like we should have done at Christmas. We stayed as long as Jacob made me and left as soon as we could, not because we didn't want to be there, but because the people we cared about were here, and sitting there playing happy families with a whole bunch of people coupled up isn't exactly my idea of a good time.

Tino and Leo take seats just inside the doorway, and more than once I check the time, wondering where the hell Ivy is.

Sophie tells me about the new office space she's got at Barrett Enterprises, and how proud Dad would be of the way Andrew's finally getting his act together and leading the teams. Apparently, he wasn't happy about having to take over, and it's caused a bit of friction. Not least because one of their biggest clients is Carlos's family, and we can all assume that money isn't coming from anywhere legitimate now.

I guess he's been inducted into the way of the world now, too. Oh, to have been a fly on the wall for some of their conversations.

But it's interesting to listen to her and hear the bits she skims over or doesn't quite explain fully. The background for which she doesn't think I know or understand. They're dangerous—Italian Mafia, whatever the hell that entails—and it's hidden in all the tiny things she's not saying.

"So, like a restaurant or something?" Ivy asks, her voice carrying from the hallway as a door closes.

"Do whatever you like, wherever you like. I honestly don't care anymore," Aimee replies, their voices getting closer.

"It's supposed to be a team effort. A collaboration," Ivy argues as the room falls quiet, all of us invested in this debate. "You've got to have some input."

Ivy stops in the doorway, her sentence trailing off as her gaze narrows, going straight to Sophie's hand on my forearm, then my eyes, and back, Something that looks a lot like jealousy flickers over her features.

"Sorry, I didn't realise we were interrupting," Aimee says, stepping back as she eyes Tino warily.

I get it. He's a big guy, dark hair, covered in tattoos, with a glare that would make even the strongest man think twice, but he seemed nice enough at Christmas. Just a bit quiet, I guess.

Sophie continues animatedly explaining something about the dance school Carlos's sister runs over in Italy, romanticising the whole thing, I'm sure, as Aimee backs away slowly, and Ivy's gaze narrows further. Her jaw clenches in determination before she marches in, placing herself comfortably on Leo's lap. He wraps his arm around her waist as he breathes her in. That fucker.

She turns up late, looking pissed off and jealous as hell, then has the audacity to flaunt this shit. She's got to be kidding.

"Shall we make a move, then?" I ask when Sophie finally takes a breath, standing and taking her hand to help her up. I have no idea what she's been going on about since Ivy walked in, all my attention being diverted to the woman currently glowering at me like she wishes she could cause me physical bodily harm from nothing but her mind powers. Thank God she can't.

"If we're all here now," Carlos comments, watching our interactions with interest.

Ivy's eyes flare, her irritation brewing at nothing more than the contact of Sophie's fingers on mine. There's nothing sexual about it—she's my damn sister—but I'm not the only one able to smell the jealousy teaming from her. Even Leo chuckles.

"Wyatt can't make it tonight. He's got an assignment to finish," Leo tells Carlos, standing and tucking Ivy under his arm.

"Go where?" Ivy asks, confused.

"To dinner."

"Dinner, like this?" she asks, gesturing to the jeans and shirt she's wearing, seemingly horrified.

Why, I have no idea, because in nothing more than her casuals she looks stunning. Maybe not 'just walked off the beach and sun-kissed' like Sophie, but the denim hugs her arse like I wish I could, the top snug around her ample tits before fluttering down in a way that is supposed to be careless, yet just looks amazing. She looks perfectly fuckable first thing in the morning, with her hair sticking out at every angle, and sleep confusing her words, so standing here looking gorgeous, I have no idea what the issue is.

"There's a pizza place not far from here. It's hardly silver service, so I wouldn't worry about it," I reply with a smile, offering my hand as I attempt to alleviate her concerns… *and* get her away from Leo.

Instead, she looks at it with disdain before shoving her hand in Leo's and turning towards the door.

"Introductions before we go would be helpful I suppose," I say, stopping Ivy in her tracks. "Ivy, this is Tino Conti, Carlos Mariotti, and Sophie Barrett, my sister."

Her unimpressed glare comes straight to mine. "You ought to have led with that," she clips out before turning to smile at Sophie and Carlos. "I'm Ivy. It's nice to meet you. Unfortunately, our host for the afternoon didn't bother to mention you were coming, otherwise I'd have been better prepared. I hope you haven't been waiting for me."

"Not at all," Sophie replies with an amused smile, patting her hand against my chest and whispering as she passes. "I like this one."

"You and me both," I say quietly before turning back to Ivy. "I added it to your online calendar. Are you still okay driving?" I ask Leo.

"Sure," he nods.

It's not that I wouldn't rather drive myself, but I may need a drink to get through this. We all might.

"Shall we?" Leo asks, leading the way while the six of us make our way through the entranceway and boot room, heading to the garage as Oliver comes in, an interested look lingering as we pass.

"Is it always this busy here?" Sophie asks.

"Well, there are eight of us, plus the occasional guest," Ivy explains over her shoulder, tucked into Leo's side. "So, yeah, I guess so. Man, I was totally freaking out about sharing an apartment with four other people, and look at me now." She barks out an amused laugh, shaking her head, revealing an admission I'd never realised before.

"Only child?" Carlos asks, Tino holding the door open for us.

"How'd you know?" Ivy asks over her shoulder with a smile.

"Just a hunch. Between family, friends, colleagues, and the strays that Tia finds, there's always someone coming or going at ours," he replies with a grin. "Give Tino the address and we'll see you there."

Ivy and I climb into Leo's Lexus whilst he gives them the address and basic directions. Tension ripples in the air between us, and just as I'm considering daring to ask her if there's a problem, Leo jumps in and backs out, leading the way as their SUV follows us closely.

I wait until we're out on the main road, the campus disappearing behind us before asking, "Still mad at me?"

"Who said I'm mad?" Ivy flicks her hair over her shoulder and looks out of the window.

"Uh, your face," I reply. It's something Jacob and I have said to each other time and time again to get us over whatever argument or miscommunication we were stewing on.

"Give over." She laughs, the sound tinkling in the enclosed car. "I come in to find some beautiful woman fawning all over you. What am I supposed to think?"

"That I'll do whatever it takes to get Jacob back, but that does not include seducing my sister." I shudder just thinking about it. Of course, she's beautiful, smart, whatever, but no. Just no. "I put all the notes in your calendar."

"Sorry, I honestly haven't checked it. You could have been waiting for me indefinitely," Ivy says.

"We'd have found you sooner or later," Leo adds with a smile, holding her hand over the central console.

"Okay, well, fill me in. What's going on?" she asks, looking at him with stars in her eyes.

"You know we learnt stuff about our families, and about our history on New Year's Eve?" I ask.

She nods, turning to catch my gaze, concern swirling through the depths of her eyes.

"Well, one of the things I found out is that my sister's fiancé is more than just some Italian businessman my family have been friends with for my entire life. He's dangerous, and he's got connections that will hopefully know how to get Jacob back, or at least get us all through. I don't know what or how, but it's got to be worth a shot," I admit.

"Oh."

"I can't just sit here and hope for the best. I need to do something. Wyatt's got people asking questions, but it's going to take time, and what's going on whilst we wait?"

"I get that, but why are *we* here?" she asks.

"Because Leo's got dark connections, too." He catches my gaze in the rearview mirror before concentrating on the road. "I just needed you."

"He's going to be okay," she says, and I realise how much of my fear must be on my face.

"Well, Carlos would do anything for Sophie, and I don't doubt for one second that she'd do anything for either of us. I mean, Jacob's her favourite little brother," I reply, pushing down the panic and bottling the top.

It's a running joke, but it doesn't help.

"He is," Leo agrees with a nod. "She said as much earlier on. It's a good job it wasn't Nick who lost because then he'd be fucked."

I scoff out a laugh, and it feels good to have someone else in on the joke. Being apart from him is driving me insane. I need to know he's okay and coming back to us in one piece. I don't know how much more of this separation I can take.

"Now, we just have to figure out how to explain all this without me losing my shit," I ponder aloud as we pull in, the other blacked-out SUV parking beside us. "And quickly."

After jumping out, I open Ivy's door and hold my hand out for her, revelling in the way she looks at me before climbing out herself. Well, at least I don't have to worry about how she feels anymore.

"You'll find the right words, don't worry," she whispers. "And if you get stuck, you've got us here, too."

"Thank you."

I don't know why I'm nervous about meeting with them. It's not just because Carlos and Tino are dangerous. I've been living with Leo for months on end, and we've seen firsthand just how volatile *his* father is. Maybe it's because this feels like a failure on my part. Maybe it's because I couldn't keep my brother safe and now he's lost to us. Or maybe it's just because I've got to tell my sister we're in over our heads.

Whatever it is, the six of us make our way inside before getting settled at a table at the back without much fuss. The conversation flows easily as we order food and drink, until…

"So, are you going to tell my why we're here at some point, or am I just supposed to guess?" Sophie asks astutely.

"Talk about throwing it out there," I grumble, attempting to buy myself some time to find the right words. "What do you know about Pendleton Prep?"

"You and Jacob go there," Sophie replies, confusion flashing across her face.

"And The Sect. Do you know what that is?" I ask as Ivy's fingers twin with mine beneath the table.

Sophie shakes her head, but Carlos tilts his head, recognition flickering over his darkened features. His eyes narrow, and my mouth dries up, all the words disappearing as I flounder with no idea how to explain this to her.

"It's taken me a minute to figure this all out, too, but let me give you the crib notes version," Ivy says, stepping in. "The Sect is some kind of secret society, and they pick their members through bloodlines, like Leo's and, uh, yours. They put their recruits through some kind of initiation challenge type thing at Pendleton Prep."

"Right," Sophie says, either not buying it or not following.

"Jacob and me, Leo and Wyatt, and the rest of the guys

at the house are all involved in an induction of sorts, and we have to pass certain challenges to stay in," I explain, swallowing thickly as I pull at my collar. "Jacob lost the last one."

"So, that's why he wasn't at the house earlier on, because he's not allowed to be there anymore? That seems a touch extreme," Sophie says with the shake of her head. "Is he at least allowed to join us for dinner?"

My mouth hangs open, the words dead on the tip of my tongue. How the hell can I explain this?

"Amore," Carlos says, taking Sophie's hand off the table and wrapping it comfortingly in his, forcing her confused gaze to meet his sympathetic one. He knows who The Sect is. He knows what this is about, and the danger we're all in right now. "You don't cross The Sect, amore. If Jacob has failed one of these challenges, he might be—"

"He's not," I interrupt, cutting him off before the words tumble from his lips. "He's okay. He's alive, as far as I know."

"What?" Sophie gasps, reading between the lines.

"Ten of us started, and only three will finish. We are down to the last four now," Leo explains from my side.

"I know Jacob is alive, but how long that will last, and what will happen, I don't know," I admit, pushing down the fear to get to the point. "I need your help."

"What on earth do you think I can do?" Sophie asks incredulously, throwing her hands in the air.

"It's not your help we're looking for," Leo says, glancing at Carlos and Tino.

"I recently learnt a few things about your *family*

connections." Yay for secret societies and their lies and deceit. "I was hoping you might be able to find something, do something," I say, catching Carlos' gaze.

Our food arrives, and the table falls quiet while we all digest what's just been said.

I've had days to stew on it, while Sophie's had nothing more than minutes. Still, my sister's stunned silence is unexpected, although it shouldn't be.

"Leave it with me," Carlos replies, nodding pensively. "And you're sure he's still…"

"Yes. Wyatt said his bracelet is still moving around, so he's not, you know, gone-gone," I reply. Not yet anyway.

"Hang on a minute," Sophie interrupts. "If you know where he is, why aren't we just going to get him?" she asks, looking from Carlos to Leo to me. "How the hell did this even happen?"

"The Sect is complicated," Carlos replies. "You couldn't walk in and take him any easier than you could wonder into a room and take Tino out of it. Can you imagine how that would go? What recompense there would be? No, that wouldn't do at all."

I guess blood oaths aren't just for the secret societies of this world.

"And you," Sophie says, gesturing to Ivy. "How do you fit into all of this?"

"The Angels are usually used to keep the Devils in line, from what I can gather," Leo explains before Ivy has chance to reply. "Things haven't gone to plan for them this year. We've made things… complicated."

"Complicated?" Sophie asks, looking from one of us to

another.

Ivy's hand squeezes mine on my thigh, giving me the comfort I need to get through this.

"Yes. Complicated. Leo and Jacob are together, but they're also with Ivy, Wyatt, and me," I admit, with no idea how this is going to go over.

"Great." Sophie sighs, rolling her eyes. "It's good to know it's not just my well laid plans the two of you are forever making a mess of, I suppose." She pushes her food around her plate before giving up and rubbing her temples. "I just… no, I don't want to know."

"When your mother mentioned the two of you were going to Pendleton Prep, I made a few enquiries," Carlos admits. "She sounded way too invested for this to be something innocuous. I knew about the link, about the potential… aftereffects. I wasn't expecting the two of you to need bailing out, but I'll find out what I can."

"Because, of course, you knew," Sophie blusters, her face now far from the professional like the rest of the world usually sees. "How could you not tell me about this?"

Yes, because they're intertwined now. A retribution given in conjunction with her new famiglia links, indeed.

"There was no need to worry you about it." Carlos shrugs as he eats before pushing the plate away. "You lot need to come to Italy at some point. I have no idea how you can pass this off as pizza. It's nothing more than a sloppy, greasy mess."

He's right, and nobody looks to be in the mood to eat anyway.

"We're down to the last four," Leo repeats. "Almost at

the end."

"And Wyatt, the guy with the tracking bracelets? He's what? Family, friend, support?" Tino asks.

"He's a Devil, too. Wyatt Chambers," I reply. He's wrapped up in this with us as well.

"Ah." Tino nods knowingly. "Gotcha."

"What does all this mean for Jacob?" Sophie asks. "And you if you don't make it through this finale?" She takes a large sip of her wine before continuing. "They've got to know that they can't just sequester some of the biggest names around and then have them never come back, surely?"

I don't have an answer for her. None of us do.

Ivy didn't visit Tamsin's family over Christmas, and they haven't reached out to her. Hell, she can't even call them because her number's blocked, which means we have no idea how this works on the other end.

"It won't come to that," Carlos says placatingly. "Leave it all with me."

"Do you have people asking questions?" Tino asks Leo.

"Yeah, I'm waiting to hear back, but I've put feelers out," Leo replies. "How did you know?"

"We've worked with your father before," Tino replies, swirling the drink around his glass. "I guess the apple doesn't fall far from the tree."

Apparently, Leo's father turned up at the old church when I went to The Sect. He saved our arses, too, by all accounts. I don't remember it. The whole thing is a blur, which is probably for the best, from what I can gather.

"There are oaths in place we can't interfere with, but I'll

find out what I can and see what can be done," Carlos says, taking Sophie's hand in his again.

"If they hurt him…" Sophie starts, her eyes watering.

Thank God she doesn't know what I did and the state I was in when they picked me up off the concrete.

"They have no reason to. He's a good kid," Tino says.

Carlos, his sister Tia, and their family have been around for most of my life. Their mother is best friends with mine. His father is likely to be the contact that linked my father with the mafia in the first place. At that thought, something else pings into the forefront of my mind.

"You probably won't remember, but you guys have met Ivy before," I say, thinking of one of the other things I learnt at New Year.

"They have?" Ivy asks, her confusion clear.

"Is everything okay with your food?" the waiter asks, interrupting and hovering beside us, looking at the mostly uneaten pizza.

"Yeah, we're just having some tricky conversations," Leo explains quickly. "Can we just grab some more drinks. No one is going to finish that."

"Uh, of course," the waiter says, picking up the closest plates and disappearing.

"So, come on. We've met before," Ivy prompts, turning in her seat and looking at me expectantly.

"Yeah, at one of the summer parties when Jacob and I were about eight, I think. We went to play hide and seek, then Jacob told everyone I was at the bathroom, and you never came looking for me," I explain.

"No idea." Carlos shrugs.

"Well, Ivy was there, and she was busy wandering around the gardens whilst I was hiding. I showed her the playground, and she fell off the climbing wall and hurt her knee," I say.

"Oh, yes, I remember that," Ivy says excitedly. "It just needed a plaster and then I was going to come and find you, but my father said it was time to leave, and I never got the chance to thank you."

"So, *we* didn't actually meet her then," Sophie says.

"Well, okay, no, not that time, but if she's been to our house, there's a good chance she'll have been other times, too. Hell, her parents are probably on your donators list."

"Donators for what?" Ivy asks, her head tilting in interest.

"I've recently taken over my mother's work and have expanded the philanthropic arm of Barrett Enterprises," Sophie explains proudly, and rightly so.

Our mother has put the bare minimum into that for years. With Sophie's organisational skills and huge heart, I have no doubt it will flourish.

"Wow," Ivy says as the waiter clears the last of the plates and refills the glasses. "So, if one were to be coordinating a charity event imminently, then you would be super useful."

"Yep," Sophie replies with a smile. "Is that what you and your friend were talking about at the house? You were looking for a restaurant or something."

"It is," Ivy admits, squeezing my hand.

"Your disgruntled friend," Carlos comments, and Ivy nods.

"Then, I'm sure we can work something out," Sophie

agrees with a nod. "Let's book a date in the diary and we can coordinate properly, but you do need to check the calendar."

"I will," Ivy replies with a smile, something akin to hope shining on her face.

"And nobody gives a shit that we've met before?" I ask, looking from one person to the next.

It sent me into a complete tailspin that night, knowing that we'd met before, and I hadn't remembered. Thinking our entire relationship could have been micromanaged and concocted by someone else, but nobody else seems to care.

"I honestly don't remember. No offense," Sophie says with a shrug of her shoulders.

"The only person who ever held my interest over here is this one," Carlos says, placing a kiss on the back of my sister's hand. "I'm sorry, but I don't remember, either."

"Helpful." I turn to Ivy, praying I'm not the only one rocked by this new information.

"I remember the party you're talking about, and I think I still have a scar from it," Ivy says, rubbing her knee absentmindedly. "But it was a long time ago, and I'm not sure we ever came again. At least, I didn't. It's entirely possible my parents did, and I was just left with Tamsin and her family or something."

"It stands to reason really. Nothing ever seems to be quite what we expect," Leo comments idly.

Isn't that the fucking truth?

FIVE

Ivy

The cold winter wind rushes around the carpark as we say goodbye to Sophie, Carlos, and Tino.

"I'll get those forms sent over in the car, and then we can Zoom or something if you need anything else," Sophie says, releasing me from her arms after our hug goodbye.

"Thank you so much. That's amazing," I reply as Nick wraps his arms around her, twirling her around before dropping her back on the ground beside Carlos.

"And you'll both come?" I clarify again.

"I don't think we have plans to go back to Italy any time soon. Just coordinate with Sophie, and she'll make sure I'm available," Carlos replies with a nod.

Awesome.

One potential investor and someone who actually knows what she's doing to help me out. Now just to sort out the rest of it.

Carlos and Nick whisper to each other whilst we all say goodbye, and eventually, Leo, Nick and I find ourselves back in the silence of the car, making our way back to

Pendleton Prep.

"Well, that was a lot," I admit. "But it sounds like positive progress."

"They're not going to be able to get Jacob out, though," Nick says with a heavy sigh, his head resting in his hand, elbow propped on the car door.

"These kinds of places take blood oaths pretty seriously," Leo agrees with a nod. "I guess I didn't when we took them."

"Me neither," Nick admits.

We didn't exactly have much time to process it the other night, but I'm reasonably sure all the attending Angels were aware just how seriously this is being taken.

"They'll do what they can, and everyone is working on it," I say reaching around the chair to rest my hand on him somewhere, anywhere. "At least we know he's alive and safe. Someone will come up with something."

The amount of people we have asked favours of and that are looking into ways to get Jacob out of this safely is unreal. There has to be a way."

"And good news for your fundraiser, too," Leo adds. "Hopefully, Sophie can help you out with getting that all set up."

"That would be amazing. Trying to get everyone to work together is proving to be an issue, and it's like Aimee doesn't even want to be here anymore. It's just really hard right now, that's all," I admit quietly.

I know it's not the same for me as it is them. Hell, Jacob is Nick's twin brother. It's nowhere near the same. But I'd got used to having him around, asking questions, calming the tension with nothing more than a hand on Leo's shoulder or a look in Nick's direction. He held us together much more than any of us realised until his calming presence was no longer there.

"Yeah," Nick agrees with a sigh. "I know that meeting today was just to talk, but it fucking sucks that Jacob isn't coming back with us tonight."

My heart clenches, and I want to reach out and hold him. The vulnerability he's kept hidden away for so long is finally visible, and he's alone.

"I know, man. I know," Leo agrees.

Sadly, the news isn't any better when we get back to the house.

Wyatt hasn't heard anything, and there's no note from Leo's contacts, either. The mood is sombre, and that carries over into dinner and the stilted conversations that we manage throughout. Eventually, the four of us end up wrapped up on the sofa in our room, with God only knows what playing on the TV.

"Pass me that notebook, will you?" I ask Leo, gesturing to the pad and pen on the coffee table.

He hands it over silently, watching me with interest.

"Right, ten started, and three end. Tell me all. Who, when, why, and how? We're going to figure this out," I decide.

"Huh?" Nick asks, peeking out from under the edge of the blanket.

"Turn this off," I say, gesturing to the TV. It's time we take back our control. "You guys have done what you can for the situation we're in, but I think if we look at what's happened so far, we might be able to rule in or rule out some ideas for the final challenge. What do you think?"

"I think attempting to outsmart a society like The Sect is pretty futile, but let's see what we can come up with," Wyatt agrees, sitting up.

"Okay, first round. I don't even know what his name was, but that was a physical challenge before the start of classes," Leo says.

"Okay." I nod, writing it down.

"Then we had to clean up the campus after the mixer," Nick says, looking at Leo as something unspoken passes between them. "Nobody left, but we got our masks and rules, and George opened his mouth and got his leg snapped in half."

Swallowing, I add it to the list.

"Then it was the escape rooms, where we lost Emmerson," Leo says. "But from what I remember that might have been justified."

"Justified?" I ask, unable to hide the horror in my tone.

"Well, George went before that, but he tried to shove me back through the door with the man that had just thrown a knife past Jacob's head," Wyatt explains.

"He did what? Jesus." I sigh, shaking my head as I attempt to wrap my brain around everything they've been through.

"So, it was George first because of the rules, then Emmerson," Leo confirms, gesturing to the notepad on my lap.

"What were the rules he broke? The ones you were given after the mixer?" I ask, turning the page.

"Look after the Angels, support each other, no more than two drinks at events, and we have to clear up after all the parties," Nick rattles off.

"I always thought you were very clean," I comment idly, attempting to remember any of them cleaning up at events.

"We got our masks, too, and found out about you guys being important. I think that's everything," Wyatt adds as they all pause, thinking.

"I guess the next thing that happened was that guy threatening Stephanie, and the rampage Oliver went on after," Nick says breaking the silence.

"That wasn't a challenge, though. That was just us working together. The next official loss was Taylor," Wyatt says, finishing his sentence in nothing more than a whisper. "That was because of the rules, and clearly an example was being made about, or for, the Angels, too."

"Next, Jasper at the puzzle and cubes thing, then Jacob for New Year Revelations," Nick rushes out.

Writing it all out may have been a mistake. It's just a categorised list of losses, one after another, after another. How are we supposed to see the wood for the trees here?

"So, we're clear on the rules, and nobody has any strikes in that regard, do they?" Wyatt asks, shuffling in closer.

They all shake their heads.

"If we just look at the tasks and not the names, so far there has been physical strength, problem solving, logical thinking, and I suppose emotional regulation… maturity? Being able to keep going despite learning stuff you never really needed to know," Leo says with a faraway look as a shiver ripples over his body.

"And your rules all seem to be about trust and loyalty. So, where does that leave us?" I ask. "What else could be coming your way?"

"I have no fucking idea," Nick says, exasperation tumbling from him as he throws himself back against the cushions.

"Someone open Google. What are the most common secret society initiations or mafia inductions? A search engine is bound to have answers to this," I say.

Leo side-eyes me warily but picks up his phone before typing away. Wyatt and I wait on bated breath, while Nick is clearly filled with resignation. Leo's eyes widen as he reads and scrolls, not a word tumbling from his lips as the seconds tip by until, with a sigh, Wyatt reaches for his phone, ready to find his own answers.

"Don't bother. There's everything from ritual sacrifices over ancient texts through to recitation. It's probably all bullshit, anyway, too," Leo grumbles, throwing his phone down in irritation.

"But we know where you've been and what you've come through now. We've gone over the rules that need to be followed to keep everyone safe, and that's a good start, right?" I ask, looking from one to another.

"Whatever they're going to get us to do next is going to be big, showy, and it won't play into Oliver's strengths. They've got the three they were looking for. We just have to keep our noses clean and get from here to there," Leo says.

"We've got this," Wyatt agrees before turning to look at Nick. "Can you hold it together?"

All eyes fall to where Nick sits beside me, his head against the back of the sofa and eyes closed, with his arm slug across his forehead, the weight of the world pressing down on his shoulders—something we can all feel right now.

"I failed again, huh? I'm the weakest link. It should have been me," he admits on a whisper, causing all the air to leave my lungs.

My heart breaks seeing the torture he's going through. Sure, we were just meeting his family to ask for help, but he was clearly hoping for more, however subconscious that hope may have been.

"You'd have opened your fucking mouth and found yourself shot by now, and you damn well know it," Wyatt clips out. "Jacob is the only one who has a chance at weathering whatever it is they're going to throw at him, and he'll come out stronger for it."

His words hang in the air until Leo asks. "Do you want to punch it out?"

"I still fucking ache from this morning," Nick replies with a grumble.

The gym has become their new favourite spot.

Wake up without Jacob? Let's spar.

Empty space at breakfast? Cool. Weights.

He should be in a class right now? Cardio it is.

If they're not careful, they're going to be worn out when their time comes.

"I'll join you," Wyatt offers, clearly feeling the weight of the moment as he stands. "Going through all this has got inside my head."

"Cool. You guys okay here?" Leo asks.

I nod, a small smile playing on my lips as Wyatt kisses my head, then the two of them make their way out.

"I made a batch of those bath salts this morning. They're in a blue box on the shelf if you need them. I figured if we were going to keep up this pace, they'd come in useful," Wyatt admits before they slip out of the door.

Ruminating over the notes in my lap is getting us nowhere fast. Now we have to hold steady and keep moving forward. Give the people we've reached out to time to do what they can, and hope Jacob's not too broken at the end— pray we all aren't. But if Nick's hurting right now, I can do something about that.

Sliding the pad and pen onto the coffee table, I quickly head to the huge tub in the bathroom, set the hot water running, and throw in a couple of handfuls of the salts that Wyatt made up before tying my hair up and out of the way. Something floral permeates the air as the steam rises, and I set the lighting to low.

I get that this separation is hard for Nick, but he's not alone, and we can carry him through this.

He's exactly where I left him when I return, his arm draped over his face, avoiding the entire world. One eye cracks open as I step between his spread legs, running the palm of my hand up each of his thighs and pressing my lips gently to his.

"Come and relax with me."

He rolls his eyes but accepts my outstretched hands before following me through to the bathroom. I don't know whether it's his silence that's more concerning or the easy acquiescence. This man would have argued that the grass was purple and the sky was yellow if I'd said different... until a few days ago, anyway.

Steam billows from the tub, and I top it up with cold water, swishing it around with my fingertips before flicking the droplets at his face with a smile. The anticipation builds as I peel each item of clothing off one by one, his heated gaze burning a path over my skin.

Nick and I have always been drawn to each other, two magnets unable to resist the pull, but in the wake of everything else going on around us, the moment is heated, sensual, charged but not volatile. Not until my toe breaks the surface of the water, and I step in, waiting to see what he says, what he does.

Sliding his shirt over his head, he eventually drops it to the floor, those six-pack abs no longer black and blue from the beating at the hands of The Sect but sculpted to perfection after the hours and hours spent in the gym. The rest of his clothes land at his feet quickly, and soon he's throwing his socks down before stepping in behind me.

It's a huge tub, with easily enough space for four of us to relax, so he could have chosen to be elsewhere, to put space between us, but his hands come to my hips, and his lips find my shoulder as he pulls my back to his chest and sits, resting back as the water cascades over us both, savouring the silence.

There have been so many words said, requests for help sent and time spent recapping, that I guess it's nice to just sit and be, however hard the actual waiting is. My fingers draw pattens across his thigh, the muscles moving beneath as his hands roam and explore the planes of my body.

He's seen it before, many times from plenty of different angles, but there's something so much more intimate about his delicate touches in the dimly-lit room.

"Do you think Jacob's okay?" he eventually whispers.

"Yes," I admit. "The Sect have gone to great lengths to secure their bloodline members. They wouldn't risk that, risk him."

It was a long time ago when Wyatt showed me the cemetery and the garden of remembrance: the unmarked grave for the ashes and remnants of those who didn't make it through. I never understood. It never felt real. Not until I saw them murder Charlotte in cold blood.

A not so insignificant part of me had been holding on to the hope that Tamsin would turn up one day, but not anymore.

"You think?" he asks, drawing me back into the moment.

"I do." I nod, turning in his grip to straddle his hips.

I'm not sure what he's looking for. Hope, love, answers… anything other than the soul crushing emptiness that seeps from his every pore.

I trace my fingers along his hairline, past his ears, and along his jaw, holding his face in my hands as his hazel gaze searches deep into my soul.

"How can we go forward without him?" he asks.

"We won't need to. Jacob is safe somewhere else, but we are moving on this path, while Jacob is on that one for now. If we let this take us under, those paths might not ever merge. So, we go forward together, and we wait for the moment that brings us back as one."

Because I have to believe that moment will come. We all do.

"Back as one," he repeats.

His eyes flutter as I slide my fingers through his hair, my nails raking against his scalp as his dick twitches behind me and his lips press against mine. The second his tongue tangles with mine, it's like a switch has flicked, and need crawls through my veins.

We can't change what's happened, but we can certainly live for the moment, because it's becoming clearer and clearer that the next ones aren't promised.

His huge hands grip my hips, slowly grinding me back and forth against his thickening length, a rumble creeping from his chest.

"Fuck, Ivy," he rasps, tipping his head back as the two of us drag heavy air into our lungs.

Adept fingers pinch and pull my nipple, the other hand sliding up to caress my breast while the water laps between us when his tongue finally joins in the action.

Everything outside of this room ceases to exist. There's no secret society picking us off one by one. No threat hiding behind every corner. There's just this need coiling every muscle tighter and tighter, wrapping around every molecule as I lift myself up, guiding him to my aching core before pushing downwards again.

Our moans mingle and echo from wall to wall once I get myself fully seated, each achingly delicious inch setting my body on fire. My core clenches around him as his lips crash against mine, his hands threading through my hair, gripping and pulling me to him. His hips roll beneath me. My knees dig into the ceramic of the bath when I remember to move, lifting and grinding—a frenzy of feeling. Water splashes over the side, pooling around the tub when, nothing more than minutes later, an orgasm hits me like a train, crashing into me with force. Nick quickly follows as his thrusts stutter and then stop.

Our panted breaths are the only sounds as I move off him, my knees protesting the motion until I get seated and he drags my back up against his chest, pouring water over my shoulders as his heartbeat thunders behind me. The two of us relax into the moment, enjoying the reprieve while it lasts.

SIX

Leo

wareness prickles the back of my neck as I slide my tablet back into my bag, turning but not catching anyone's gaze.

Someone is watching me.

"An early finish. I'll take that for the first day back," Ivy says with a smile, clearly enjoying not having to rush from one class to the next.

It doesn't help that this professor runs late nine times out of ten, leaving me to rush her from one class to the next, but today, it seems, we get a reprieve.

"Absolutely."

"Are you going home from here?" she asks as the two of us head out, following the handful of other students from the airy lab.

"I'm not sure," I admit, uncertain when the big house at the bottom of the road became 'home'. "I'm thinking about taking a drive."

Nobody is paying us any attention, what with everyone heading to their next lecture or apartment, lost in their own business. Everyone except for a group of guys mucking around in the atrium, their gym bags in hand.

"Shall we wait inside?" I offer, looking at the dank winter drizzle through the huge glass windows. We're early so Nick isn't here yet, and I could walk her all the way to the class, but she's got information I think I need. "Which school did you say the Little Sisters attend? Somewhere nearby, right?"

"South Beach," Ivy replies as we drop onto the bench by the doors, close enough to see when Nick arrives, but far enough away to avoid the draft. "Why?"

Nerves eat at my insides, and I bite my bottom lip, not sure if I should tell her now or wait for the fall out, if it ever comes.

"It's been more than a week," I admit quietly, not giving her the full explanation.

Her smile drops, and her hands reach for mine, acting as a balm that soothes the angry beast ready to start rattling cages and looking for answers in all the wrong places.

"I know this is hard."

"A week," I repeat, cutting her off. "What the hell could happen to him in a week?"

My mind can picture exactly the things that can be done in a week. Beaten. Starved. Tortured. I've done it all, and worse.

"Wyatt said—"

"I know… he's alive," I say, cutting her off with a sigh.

We've been through this a lot over the last few days. If it's not me, it's Nick, checking and re-checking the tracking app. Waiting, praying, and hoping. It's driving me insane.

"We'll hear something soon, I'm sure."

She catches my gaze, drawing my thoughts back to her

and away from the depraved things I've done in a week—things that could be being done to the man I care so much about right now. She squeezes my hands before her gentle touch brushes along my jaw, holding me captive, attempting to impart her strength straight into my veins.

And it worked at first. A look, a touch, a calming moment. They were enough to quiet the beast inside, but not anymore. Now it's had enough of watching and waiting. Now it demands answers or blood.

"Have you heard anything back from…" Her question trails off, neither of us sure how much can be said here.

Disappointment fills me as I shake my head.

The first thing I did when we got back on New Year's Day was to put a request in for Dex or Blaise to get in touch or help—red bulbs for the win—but I don't know if they've even seen them, and despite the red roses I sent to their house, I haven't heard anything, and it's getting desperate.

Nick knocks on the glass behind us, jolting us from the moment as he taps his watch impatiently.

Yeah, we've been waiting for *you*, dipshit.

"Sorry, I've got to go. Why not hit the gym for a bit?" Ivy offers.

"Yeah, I might do that."

Her lips press against mine briefly, nothing more than a tease before she's walking away, heading to her next class with Nick.

Fuck. It hurts to look at him and see all the similarities and differences. The pain that lances through him just like it does me. I can't do this anymore.

Grabbing my bag, I sling it on my shoulder and head

out into the freezing cold to make my way to the car. Ivy's stupid ex holds the door for me, heading out with his friends at the same time. He knows better than to speak to me after the shit he tried to pull with Ivy, and he's soon dropping his gaze and scurrying away as I make my way to the car, jump in, and lock the doors. I pull up the GPS and programme the address in, checking the arrival time of my destination.

Perfect. I'll get there with twenty minutes to spare.

The engine rumbles to life beneath me as I turn her around and make my way to the main gates.

I could head back to the house and hit the gym again, but I think the six miles on the treadmill I did before breakfast were enough to take the edge off, and there's no more relief to be found there.

Now I need answers.

Traffic holds me up, and I almost panic that I've missed my opportunity when I finally pull up outside the quiet building, but when I doublecheck the time, I know I'm safe. They're still here.

Second thoughts swirl through my mind. I shouldn't be here. This is stupid, dangerous, and all the things I said I'd never do or be.

But when the bell rings, the doors open, and a few minutes later, the students of South Beach High file out. Class by class, group by group. The jocks. The nerds. Gaggles of girls, but none of them are the one I'm looking for.

I've almost given up hope when I spot her sliding out of the doors, giving stink-eye to the girls ahead of her as she pushes her bag up her shoulder. She's not expecting me, wouldn't even know what to look for if I'd had some way to inform her that I was coming, but my whistle echoes across the road, garnering more than just her attention.

After spotting me and shaking her head, she attempts to walk away, pushing past the girls she was glaring at just seconds ago.

"Yo, Ruby!" I call, her name repeating from one set of lips to another as it follows her along, her classmates attempting to get her attention too.

Flash cars are no big deal around here, but my overpowered Lexus roars when I press the start button, more than willing to chase her along. Luckily, the rumble catches the attention of some guys ahead of her, and with the promise of talking engines, they drag her back towards me. She's not quite kicking, screaming, or fighting like I'm sure she could do if she wanted, but she's definitely less than impressed.

"What are you doing here?" she quips, shucking the grip of the boy who dares to run his fingers along my baby's paintwork. I notice his uniform isn't matching the rest of the ones that mill around here.

"I'm here for you. Jump in," I tell her.

With a roll of her eyes, she dumps her bag in the back and plonks herself in the passenger seat with a pout.

I spend a couple of minutes talking with my new little helpers, handing them some cash before climbing in and making my escape with Ruby in tow. Well, that went better than expected.

She doesn't look at me when we pull away from the school, but the silence is weighted.

"I don't know how you fit into this mess, but I've not heard from them. Did they get my message?" I ask, knowing she'll have answers.

Dex told me she was something to them, that she was safe and could be trusted. Now she has to prove it, but it's a redundant question anyway because I know they got the gift I sent. I got the damn delivery notification, but I've got to start somewhere.

Ruby doesn't answer, refusing to give me her attention as she stares out of the passenger window.

"Are they okay? Did something happen that means they can't come back to me? I know they're being watched, but this seems excessive," I ramble.

It's not like me to lose it, but it's been a week. A week.

"I don't know who or what you're talking about," she replies, still refusing to look at me.

Irritation bubbles beneath my skin, an itch I can't scratch as Ruby continues to deny any knowledge of Dex, Blaise, and the situation we find ourselves in. She may not be in the middle of this with The Sect like we are, but she sure as shit knows what's going on with my brothers.

"Hurting women isn't usually my go-to, but you're really starting to piss me off," I warn her, squeezing my fingers around the steering wheel as I attempt to rein in it.

"Where are you taking me?" she asks, obviously not recognising anything out of the windows as she suddenly seems to realise the danger she's put herself in.

I don't know the area very well myself, and I have no idea where she lives, but I was hoping she'd be helpful, or that the silence may have encouraged some compliance. No luck on either front, unfortunately.

Driving through the quiet streets is getting me nowhere, though, and that's the exact place I've been for the last week: nowhere. So, I pull into the next empty car park I see, turning the engine off before swivelling in my seat to face her silently.

The seconds tick by as she checks her nails and ignores me completely.

"I know a few things about you," I tell her, slinging my arm over the steering wheel to take her in properly.

She may put on a good front to the Angels, to Ivy, and when she's been around us as a group, but here, trapped in this small, enclosed space with me, it's crumbling.

"Yeah, like what?" She throws the words down like a gauntlet. Pinning me with a venomous look, she scoffs.

"I know you're nowhere near as oblivious as you'd like us to think you are. I know The Sect got you into the Little Sister programme, and that my father pays your tuition at this fancy school you hate."

"So what if he does? What's it to you?"

A million thoughts flicker through her eyes, fear and hate just two of them.

It took me a minute to put all the pieces together, finding out about her background from Ivy and Dex at Christmas. She may be something to my brothers, but she was sent here by my father.

"I know you've been spying on Ivy and me from the beginning, sending information back to my father. What I can't work out is why?"

She cocks an eyebrow, confirming nothing.

"Or how Dex fits into this whole thing, too."

Josiah has his little birds all over. While my father isn't getting updates from The Sect, or access to their surveillance, I'm sure he'll be getting information from Josiah. So, why the need to send her in, too?

"He's known for explaining himself, is he? Your father?" Ruby asks, shaking her head.

She knows as well as I do that he doesn't, but it's the crack I was waiting for. The first step on the way to an admission.

"You told him about Nick going to the church when he handed himself over. That's how he got there so quickly. But how did you know?"

It's the one thing I haven't been able to nail down. To get there at almost the same time we did means he must have been on his way for hours. He got the heads up, and we didn't. Would he have acted if I didn't call? If we didn't realise in time? Or would he have hung back and left Nick to his fate?

"You're seriously barking up the wrong tree," she argues, pushing all her real feelings deep down again.

I run the tip of my tongue against my bottom lip, pressing them together. It's been too long since I felt Jacob's lips on mine, and she's got answers I need. Reaching out, I run my fingers through the hair draped by the side of her face. Her eyes narrow, but she doesn't flinch back.

She's young and pretty, in that girl-next-door kind of way. Her brown eyes take in my every movement with suspicion, then she's swallowing thickly as I graze against the softness of her skin, grip her chin and drag her across the centre console closer to me.

"What do you think he'd say if I kissed you?" I whisper.

Her sharp intake of breath echoes in the silence, but the fear that reflects back at me is unmistakable as I plough on.

"Do you think he'd be angry with me… with you? Or do you think it would all be over? That whatever you had with him would be done and dusted with nothing more than a few words from me?"

"You wouldn't…" Tears prick in her eyes because she knows I would. My silence and the solemnity of the words that tumbled from me confirm it.

"Jacob is gone, and the only two men I've ever counted on are MIA. Do you really think I wouldn't lie to get a response? To get the help and answers I need?"

One traitorous tear slips over her lashes, anger brewing a storm in her gaze when she rips her face from my hold.

"He knows." *Dex.* "They're looking." *Dex and Blaise.* "But they can't come back to you right now," she admits, the words clearly bitter on her tongue. "He's watching them."

"My father?"

She shakes her head, sighing. "Josiah."

Of course.

My father may be the one moving the pieces on the board, but Josiah is the one watching them and keeping them in place.

"Fuck."

I don't know why I came here. What I was hoping for. Deep down I knew she couldn't have the answers I was looking for. I'm beginning to wonder if anyone does. I'm just unravelling without him, and that's not like me.

I've never relied on anyone or anything in my life. Never been able to. But in the space of less than six months, Jacob has buried himself under my skin. He's a weakness I should never had been allowed.

My hand drops to the central console between us as she angrily wipes away a tear, her own weakness revealed. Ruby may not give a flying fuck about putting herself in danger—she jumped in the car with me without much persuasion—but her relationship with the *friend* on the other end of her phone, the same one that sent her to us coded in blue? Yeah, that's important to her.

"Would you pass me my bag?" she asks sheepishly.

With a shrug, I grab it from the back seat and hand it over. She rifles through one of the pockets before pulling an envelope out and straightening the pages inside, scanning over the words before handing one sheet to me and folding the other in her lap.

"Who the hell sends letters anymore?" I ask, accepting the offered paper like a lifeline.

"People with no privacy. Just fucking read it."

The phone usually always in her hand is nowhere to be seen today. It's probably not a good sign. Neither are the nerves that eat at me as I take in the handwriting and the words on the page.

"Can't extract. Contacts in place. He needs a way in, not out."

Silently, she looks at the paper in her lap.

"So, not only did you know exactly what I was talking about, but you had the message practically on your person," I confirm, my hands shaking as adrenaline courses through me.

Ruby shrugs, looking out the passenger window again as I attempt to submerge the rage coursing through my body.

"Dex told me to trust you, did you know that? When I confronted him about the conniving little girl that had been sticking her nose in places it wasn't supposed to be, he told me I could trust you." I scoff out a laugh, shoving the paper in my pocket. "Were you even going to give me this?"

She shrugs again.

"Ruby." The word comes out in an irritated growl, and her gaze travels to me.

"No," she clips out. "The first I hear from him in days, and I'm nothing more than a messenger girl? No, I wasn't going to hand it over like the good little bitch you all treat me as."

All the bravado she's been blowing into her sails puffs out like a pin popping a balloon when she takes my obvious anger.

"Dex trusted you, defended you, and this is how you act? Do you have any idea about him at all?" I ask in disbelief.

Aside from the fact that I need this information, trust isn't something freely given in our world, it's earnt. If he gave her this, dropped it in the letterbox to her house, then she means more than I realised. She's a bigger piece in this game than I'd previously considered. She just doesn't realise it yet.

"Are you… will you tell him?" she asks nervously.

I should.

How can we trust her to go between me and Dex when she does this? How can we trust that she's not going to run back to Josiah or my father with the note, the details of it, or more?

Shit. What if she'd given this to Josiah? Then they'd have known that Dex and I were in conversation, and that we were managing to work together, despite all the things they've put in place to keep us apart. They'd also know how much more important Jacob is to me than I'd let on.

"I want to know what you know," I say.

No more lies. No more hiding. If she's in this with us, then she's in this *with* us.

"A camera was placed at the church. That's how I knew to warn them that something was happening," she admits. "Being placed with Ivy was intentional, but I don't know why."

"And Dex?"

She swallows, turning away as she fiddles with the edge of the paper in her hand before shoving it back in the envelope and her bag, and dropping the bag behind her seat as she works out what to say or how to phrase her truth.

"He's… I'm his… he's important to me, okay? I'm sorry if you needed that paper, and I'm sorry I wasn't more forthcoming. Just… just don't tell him, please." Her pleading gaze catches mine once more.

She's lucky I'm *this* me and not the one of six months ago. That one would have laughed in her face as he sealed her fate, called his brother, and caused him pain to keep him safe in the long run.

"You hear from either of them again, you call Ivy to meet. No excuses. No delays."

"Thank you." Her sigh of relief holds so much more

than she realises.

"You're on our side now, but if for one second I think you're holding back, lying, manipulating…. I won't hesitate to make that call," I promise.

Trust is earned, not given, and she's got a lot to make up for here.

Begrudgingly, she nods.

"This isn't one sided. If you need something, we've got your back, too," I add.

Surprise flashes across her features before she smiles, something like peace falling between the two of us.

"I don't know how you ended up in the middle of all this, Ruby, but if you know Dex and Blaise as well as it seems you do, then you know exactly what breaking their trust entails. Puppet or not, that shit's important."

She nods again in answer.

"And I will bury you if I find out you've double-crossed us."

It's not a threat, it's a promise, and one she fully understands if the look she gives me is anything to go by. I may be a better person now than I used to be, but that is unravelling more with every moment that passes.

"It was a mistake. I was angry. I would have handed it to Ivy when I saw her next," she admits, eyes downcast.

"And if we'd moved without that info? Found ourselves right in the shit with no way to get out… how would you have explained that?"

She's just a girl, dumped in the middle of this thing with no clue. Dex's trust is unfounded. I guess that's how tied down and desperate he is right now.

She doesn't answer, her head dropping as defeat slumps her shoulders. A black Audi pulls away when I turn the engine on and ask where she wants to be dropped off. I guess at this point, we've no choice but to stay on course and pray for the best.

SEVEN

Ivy

The band practice quietly in the corner, tuning their instruments, and running through their warmups as the front of house staff gather in a circle, going over their last-minute instructions. The room is light, bright, and everything looks fresh and clean, exactly as planned.

While flicking through the pages in my hand, I go over the name for each potential investor, reminding myself who they are and what they do, hopeful I'll remember it all when faced with them. I've been memorising this for days and days, and I've spoken with most of their assistants personally, hoping that personal touch makes a difference. Shuffling the list of lots to the front of my clipboard, I look from pedestal to pedestal, checking everything is where it's supposed to be.

The artwork Sophie donated sits beautifully on its stand, the pop of colour the perfect contrast to the black and white football jersey on the next stand—signed, of course. Gathering up a good mix of options turned out to be easier than I originally anticipated, the four of us managing to come up with a great list, with minimal crossovers.

Sure, there were one or two, and Stephanie was less than impressed at having to swap one of hers out, but any deviation from her took some strong negations on my part. Penelope was happy to go with whatever, and Aimee couldn't care less, but with Sophie's guidance, I've managed to steer us along the right path… at least that's how it feels. We're currently not in the middle of a blacked-out rave, so that feels like a win.

"Uh, we have a problem. We're one lot short," Penelope whispers in my ear, her gaze fixed on something over my shoulder.

"What?" I ask, looking down at the list, my gaze flicking from one pedestal to the next. "Everything looks to be where it's supposed to be."

"There's a provenance issue with one of Aimee's lots, but she still wants to put it in so it's on the stand."

"Issue? What kind of issue?" This was all supposed to be checked and crossed off days ago… weeks, even!

"There should be a certificate that goes alongside it, but she can't find it."

"Shit," I hiss. "Where is she?"

"Currently arguing with the auctioneer." She grimaces.

The booklets have been printed, and the paddles are being handed out in the lobby as we speak. This is not the moment for shit to hit the fan. Spotting the two of them, I go straight over, interrupting their hushed argument.

"Pull it," I say, cutting Aimee off. "If we don't have the right documentation, we can't prove it's legitimate. That being auctioned off and later proven to be a fake or a fraud would bring into question every piece we sell tonight, along with the funds procured, and the cause they're being donated to. Pull it."

"Oh, come on." Aimee sighs, throwing her hands in the air with exasperation. "We all know these *investors* aren't legit anyway. Neither is the event, or probably even the programme. It will be fine."

"We're not bringing this entire thing down just because you don't believe it's real," I argue, nodding to the auctioneer before pulling her to the side. "I don't know about you, but the people I've invited aren't looking to throw their money at fakes."

"It's not a fake. I just can't find the certificate. It's probably in one of the million boxes of paperwork my mother has stashed in her office," Aimee replies. "We'll be a lot short."

"We'll trade it out. Take that down and put it away somewhere. Did we have any back-ups?"

"Not that can be here within ten minutes or less," she replies looking anxiously at the clock. "I'm going to be one behind everyone else for the final count."

Shit. I hadn't thought about that.

"Let me think."

Penelope joins me as Aimee pulls her item from the stand, going to find somewhere safe to store it whilst the two of us brainstorm.

"Do you think her father would donate a weekend at their Italian villa?" Penelope asks.

"Or a stay at their hotel in Thailand, maybe?" I ponder.

"Don't we already have a couple of travel-based lots, though?" she asks with a cringe.

"Yeah," I reply, checking down the list. "What about… an evening in London with one of the Devils?" I ask, catching sight of one of the guys.

"Don't you need to ask them about that first?" she wonders, looking around.

"Probably. I'm sure it would be fine. Dinner and a show with one of the infamous Devils would be worth a shot though, right?" I ask.

"Wasn't there a proprietary clause in the specification somewhere?"

"I'm not pimping them out. It's just dinner. Do you think Aimee would go for it? It might be all we can cobble together at this point."

Stephanie flings the doors back, the chatter from the hall spilling through the doorway as she excitedly welcomes everyone in and directs them to her lots first.

"Well, I'll leave that with you," Penelope says as Leo comes over, his charcoal shirt sitting sinfully well on his shoulders.

A smile kicks up one side of his mouth as he pushes his dark hair back, stalking towards me like a predator, despite the weariness I see in each step.

Well, here goes nothing.

"Hey, angel," he says, pressing his soft lips to my cheek briefly. "It's looking amazing in here."

"Thanks, but I've got a problem. Is there any chance Aimee can auction off dinner and a show with you or one of the guys? We've been let down last-minute," I ask quickly. Not only because we are running out of time before everyone turns up and we have to start, but because if I don't ask it now, I'll chicken out.

"Really?" He quirks an eyebrow.

"Please." Pressing my palms together, I give him my best puppy dog eyes, praying he says yes.

"Fine." He shrugs. "I'm not sure how good company any of us would be, all things considered, but go for it."

The last four weeks have been hard. Really hard.

Leo's brothers can't get Jacob out, and Carlos's contacts haven't had any luck, either. They're keeping an eye on things, and he's safe as far as we know, but the distance and the strain is showing in a big way.

"You're amazing, thank you. I'll just let everyone know and then we can make a start of the shmoozing."

Quickly, I find both Aimee and the auctioneer and fill them in on the amendment, promising her it will all be fine. That's probably not something I should promise, but it's the best we've got right now.

Plucking a glass from a passing waiter, I then take the moment to look around. The auctioneer is placing a decorated card where Aimee's pottery used to be, and people are chatting, smiling, and generally looking to be enjoying themselves.

"You've done beautifully," Wyatt praises, his hands pressing against my arms as he comes up behind me, his soothing presence a balm I didn't realise I needed in this moment. "I know it's been a team effort and all that, but it's been a touch unbalanced in my opinion."

"You're biased," I reply with a small smile, his cologne wrapping around me. "Did you hear anything yet?"

"I've left another message, but nothing yet," he admits

quietly. "Are they here yet?"

Rather than coming in with us to set up and deal with all the final hiccups, Nick went to meet Sophie and Carlos to catch up with them before joining us with the rest of the guests.

"I haven't seen them yet, but they shouldn't be far off."

"Come on, let's get some of these people lined up for the best lots." He winks, twinning his fingers with mine before placing a chaste kiss on my cheek, then leading me to the closest group of people and introducing us.

They are two of the investors provided by The Sect, also known as Timeless Inc., and the Big Sister programme, no doubt, amongst other things. I think it's all pretty interchangeable at this point. After a couple of minutes chatting, I manage to suggest more than one item that might be their cup of tea—one of which happens to be my lot.

I'm sure Stephanie is doing nothing more than promoting her own, and whilst I understand the logic to it—lowest raiser is out after all, but that's not how I roll—I'm not going to push mine for the sake of it. I got a good balance of things, I hope. That's got to be enough.

After wishing them an enjoyable evening and the best of luck with their biddings, I catch Leo's gaze across the room, gesturing to the entrance and the familiar couple now entering, with Nick tagging along behind them.

There's something akin to determination powering each of his steps, and whilst his jaw is still harder than stone, and the smiles of Christmas seem like nothing more than a figment of my imagination, there's hope hidden in the depths of his hazel gaze.

Converging in the middle of the room, I thank Sophie again for all her help as she wraps her excited arms around me in a very familiar hug.

"You've done a fantastic job," she says with a smile before passing me over to Carlos.

"I think we've got something," Carlos whispers when he pulls me in. "No promises though." He winks as he steps back, excitement coursing through my veins.

They take a list of my lots with their numbered paddle and wander away, leaving Nick with Wyatt, Leo, me, and a million more questions that I can't possibly get answers to.

"Good news?" Leo asks, adjusting Nick's collar, fishing for the information we all want.

It would be cute, sweet, even, if it was Jacob, but Nick pins him with an unimpressed glare, letting him finish nonetheless.

"Maybe," Nick muses, looking around. "Time will tell, I suppose. I've still got a bad feeling about tonight. We're still together, right?"

He gives us nothing, instead focusing on the task at hand. Part of me wants to argue that The Sect wouldn't try something in the middle of an event we'd organised, but then that didn't stop them at New Year's…

Leo draws to my left side, Wyatt to the right as Nick blocks the path ahead, his serious gaze flickering from one of us to the next as all the unspoken words between us flicker in the air.

Stay safe.

Stay seen.

I need you.

"You've all got your bracelets on?" Wyatt asks, and we nod.

"You've got your knife?" Leo asks, the darkness he tries so hard to hide from the rest of the world coming to the fore.

"Yes, and yes," I confirm.

"It's been too long, too quiet, and these big money investors are much more involved than I'm sure we're supposed to believe," Leo says.

"Stay near, okay?" Wyatt instructs with a cursory glance.

"Is that your ex?" Leo asks, pulling a face as he glowers at someone over Nick's shoulder. "What the hell is he doing here?"

As a unit, they all turn to Spencer who's looking like a dear caught in the headlights.

"Him, I have no idea, but I did invite his parents," I reply. "There's a good chance they'll put in for one or more of these lots, and despite the douche their son turned out to be, they're good people."

"Someone needs to keep an eye on him, too, then," Wyatt says. "But not you."

"Fine, fine. Let's go and say hello and get this out of the way and then you guys can keep an eye on him. The less I have to do with him, the better."

"I'll join you," Leo says offering his arm to me. "He won't be a dick whilst I'm around."

"Yeah, why is that?" I ask as Nick and Wyatt move away, the two of them heading to chat with another group of people—someone Aimee invited, I think.

I meant to ask him ages ago how they knew each other,

how he managed to get the pompous arse to close his mouth and leave me alone in advanced bio back when we first started, when Spencer dropped a book on Leo's foot and practically ran in fear.

I guess there was something to be said for the warning he tried to give me about big, bad, scary Leo Windsor, but it's safe to say he's not the biggest threat roaming the halls of Pendleton Prep. That's got to go to the secret society who know all, see all, and hear all. At least in the houses and campus buildings, from what we can gather.

"All the things that happen at water polo stay at water polo," Leo replies cryptically. "Our paths have crossed in the past."

"Good evening, Mr Hart, Mrs Hart. Thank you so much for making the time," I say as the distance closes between us, with Spencer's eye's widening in panic before he scurries away. "Is everything okay?"

The four of us watch my ex run away like he's literally on fire, disappearing to the other side of the room, where he loiters by one of the other displays.

"Absolutely fine, darling. Spencer just needed to check something on that lot for me. How are you, anyway? You're looking gorgeous this evening. And who's your gentleman friend?" Mrs Hart asks, her interested, ice-blue gaze flicking over Leo quickly before giving me her undivided attention. "It's been too long. You should come for a round at the country club next time you're home."

"Oh, it's a bit cold for me at the moment," I reply with a smile, answering the last of the many questions I should have known she'd have. "Leo Windsor, this is Derek and

Jayne Hart. They've been good friends of my parents for a lot of years."

Leo nods, shaking their hands, even as he watches Spencer at the far end of the room.

"Lovely to meet you," Leo says.

"Windsor… Windsor? No, that doesn't ring a bell," Mr Hart says, scratching the salt and pepper hair above his ear. "What is it your father does?"

"Oh, he's got his hands in a few things," Leo replies, his attention snapping back to the couple in front of us as he sways them with a disarming smile.

"Nothing I might recognise?" Mr Hart digs.

"I would doubt it," Leo replies succinctly.

I can only assume the things Leo's father does are less than legal. We haven't delved, but you don't turn up to a secret society meeting with guns and backup unless you're dabbling in things you aren't supposed to be.

"Well, he's clearly doing well for himself if you're attending here with Spencer and Ivy-Rose," Mr Hart continues, their ridiculous need to include my middle name grating just as much as when his son does it. "And how is it you know our darling girl?"

It's much less than the third-degree Leo would likely get from my parents, but considering how Derek and Jayne had been conspiring with them for years to pair us up, it's not really much of a surprise, no matter how much off topic.

"Leo and I have a few classes together," I say, intervening. "Did you have chance to look over the lots for the evening?"

"Yes, there are definitely a couple I'd like to take home,"

Mrs Hart replies. "But I guess we'll have to see how we get on." She waves the small, white, numbered paddle between us with an excited smile.

"Well, we have a few more people to greet," Leo says, waving to someone over their shoulder, offering me an out.

"Yes, of course. Again, thank you for being here, and good luck," I add.

"Wouldn't miss it, darling," Mrs Hart replies, placing a quick air kiss to both my cheeks before we manage to extricate ourselves.

"And you couldn't think of literally anyone else?" Leo asks, a fake smile on his face.

"They were the first people that popped to mind."

Well, not quite.

The first people were my parents, but there's no way I was dragging them into the middle of this. Derek and Jayne are at least oblivious enough to miss the undercurrent, but my father? Not so much.

So, we spend the next half an hour saying hello to almost all of the guests, and making sure everyone I invited turned up—which they did—and *not* crossing paths with Spencer again.

"Ladies and gentlemen, could you please take your seats?" is called out to the room, the music petering off as the guests take their seats, with the Devils and Angels loitering to one side.

Penelope and Stephanie stand hand-in-hand, Oliver with them, as Aimee joins me and the guys, biting nervously on her bottom lip.

"Thank you for joining us this evening to raise funds for

the Big Sister programme at Timeless Inc. Let's introduce the first lot," the auctioneer announces.

Penelope takes her first item from its stand, joining the auctioneer at the front as he explains the background and accompanying itinerary for the weekend trip to Vermont before the bidding commences.

I attempt to keep track of who raised what, but by the time we make it to lot nine, I've forgotten half of the prices and mixed at least one of Aimee's with one of Penelope's in my head. I give up just in time for them to announce the last-minute change and have Aimee drag an unimpressed looking Leo to the front of the room.

"Did he agree to this?" Wyatt whispers in my ear.

Nodding, we watch Leo's familiar smile slide onto his face, ready to wow the attendees as he takes the microphone.

"This was a last-minute change, so I'm afraid I don't have any fixed plans to offer you, but what I can guarantee is an evening of fun, laughter, and amazing food. I know all about food," Leo says with a million-dollar smile. His ink creeps up the side of his neck and along the back of his hands, and as the light hits him and he brushes his hair back, he looks every bit the bad boy we know him to be.

The auction begins, the numbers starting low, but when Mrs Hart and one of the other women find themselves in a bidding war, the numbers get high quickly, with the lot finishing as one of the top earners of the evening so far.

Halfway through the event, we take a fifteen-minute repose. Mrs Hart winks my way when she catches my gaze as more servers arrive with canapés and drinks, a few of the gentlemen excusing themselves for a smoke break, but not my guys.

If there was a moment, an opportunity built into this evening for The Sect to come along and fuck this up, this would be it. So, along with Aimee, the five of us stick together, keeping an eye on the entrances with bated breath. But then the interim break comes and goes, with the auctioneer calling everyone back to order for the second half. Rather than attempting to keep a tally of who raises what, I settle in with my guys, enjoying the moment and revelling in the job we've done.

I was half expecting Liselle to turn up, but Amy has been the face of the project and has tried her hand at a lot or two. Whether that was because it was something she was genuinely interested in, or if she was just trying to bump the bids, I'm not sure, but she comes away emptyhanded at the end of the night.

As the auction draws to a close, guests are advised where to make their donation and collect their items before the music recommences and the final drinks arrive.

We've done it.

"I was struggling to keep hold of everyone's figures, but you did great." Leo winks. "You both did," he adds, looking at Aimee.

"Only because you saved my arse," Aimee replies, adjusting her blouse. "Thank you for that, by the way. I would be a million miles behind if you hadn't stepped in."

"Anytime," Leo replies, watching as Nick discreetly slides away to catch his sister, his attention diverted.

EIGHT

Nick

People mill around the open hall, a couple of them saying goodbye to Penelope as I make my way to my sister and her fiancé.

"Are you guys heading out?" I ask, pulling Sophie into my arms and resting my chin on top of her head. She hates it, but that's what family is for, isn't it?

There's something calming about the familiar feel of her in my arms. It's not the same as being near Jacob. He neutralises the nervous energy that riots through my veins in a way that not even Ivy can emulate, but it all helps, and right now, I need all the help I can get.

"We are," Carlos replies with a nod.

"Did you get what you were looking for?"

Carlos nods as Sophie begins rambling on about the beautiful sculpture she managed to win and the amount of money her painting went for. I'm not sure if Ivy realises that my sister is the artist, or if she just thinks it's one of the pieces Sophie has curated through her various artistic ventures. Either way, the two of them have done great.

I should probably extend that to the rest of the Angels team or whatever, but seen as they've been nothing but a pain in the arse over the entire thing, I don't think I'll bother.

"God knows where we're going to put it," Carlos comments, rolling his eyes behind Sophie's back. "I'll get it delivered to Italy and we can sort it once we're there. There definitely isn't a place for it in the London flat."

"I don't know. I think it would look cute on the side table in the living room," Sophie argues, peeling herself from my embrace.

"Don't worry. We'll find somewhere for it," Carlos says to me with a nod before smiling down at her, adoration in his gaze.

Our families have been friends for our entire lives, but as the youngest kids in the group, Jacob and I were often late to the party compared to the others. And once Carlos and his sister hit double digits, they weren't as interested in entertaining the family friends from London whenever we visited. So, whilst our parents have maintained their friendships over the years, we never made those same kind of relationships, and now I don't know him very well.

As adults, we knew nothing of them until my father took ill and Carlos and his father became more involved with the business side of things at Barrett Enterprises. Knowing what I know now about their mafia ties, I can kind of see why. I also understand our eldest brother's hesitance when it came to Sophie's relationship with Carlos, but he seems to be keeping her safe, and she's happy and well, and seemingly serving up as much retribution as she's taking… but I don't know that officially, either.

"We'll catch you soon," Carlos says, shaking my hand before the two of them go to collect their winnings and head home.

"You seem… lighter," Ivy says, wrapping her hands around my waist and resting her head between my shoulder blades as she breathes me in.

I know I've been hard to live with recently. Snappy, grumpy. There's been a distance growing between us all as we do everything we can think of for Jacob, but to no avail. We've watched that fiery resolve to get him back simmer and slow as the day became days, and then a week, only for it to turn into weeks.

It's not because we haven't tried. We have stayed the course, trusted, waited, pushed. But knowing he's alive somewhere isn't enough for me, Leo, or even Wyatt and Ivy. We're going through the motions, holding each other together as best we can, hoping something changes soon.

The final challenge hanging over our heads isn't helping anything either. I thought going through the past would help us to work out what's coming, but God knows what The Sect have got up their sleeves. I'm just glad I'm finally back up to weight, healthy, and breathing clearly after the run in before.

Broken ribs are a bitch, and it's taken far longer than I anticipated to heal up, but I can finally make it through a few rounds in the ring without feeling like I'm dying.

"Getting there," I reply. "Do you have a lot to do to finish up here?"

"Not really. The hotel deal with the room, and the auction house are coordinating everything else. If I remember rightly, the cars will be here in fifteen minutes."

"You two should get a room," Oliver jokes as he passes,

wiggling his eyebrows. "A bit of peace and quiet after a successful night could be just what the doctor ordered."

A break from his smug face would go down a treat, but not whilst we're still in the thick of this, still searching for my brother.

"Yeah, you look like you could sleep for a week," Stephanie adds with a smirk.

"That bad, huh?" I ask once they've moved away, watching Leo chat with the auctioneer as Wyatt talks on his phone at the other end of the room.

"You look great," Ivy says, sliding around my body until she's in front of me, her green eyes peering up at me with so much affection, I'm not sure what to do with it.

For so long, I was set on chasing her, claiming her, winning her at any cost. I guess I kind of did. I just got these two other fools and my brother in the bargain. I never thought I'd see the day she looked at me like this though. Like I hung the moon, despite being the grumpy arse she knows me to be.

"Thanks, sugar."

Before I have the chance to kiss her like I want to, Aimee is waving us over, gathering everyone together, ready for the journey home no doubt.

"Who do you think raised the most, then?" Stephanie asks. "Do you think we'll get some kind of reward for it, too? That would be cool, wouldn't it?"

I'm sure it would, but we all know that's not how The Sect works. Positive reinforcement isn't exactly their forte, and whilst I wasn't paying a whole load of attention as to who sold what, I'm reasonably sure hers weren't the biggest selling lots.

"Ooh, maybe the winner will be able to give the donation to Timeless Inc.," Aimee suggests. "You know, with one of those huge, promotional cheque things."

"You seem more interested now," Wyatt comments with the tilt of his head.

It's not that Ivy's complained about Aimee's lack of interest a lot, but every time an issue has come up, it's been linked to Aimee and something she said, did, or like tonight... didn't do.

"Yeah, well. It's done now," Aimee replies with a shrug.

Sure is, and Leo bailed her arse out. She wouldn't be joking about winnings and promotional cheques if he hadn't.

We fall into silence as we wait for the cars. Stephanie and Oliver take the first one, the girls next, as Leo, Wyatt, and I clamber into the final car. I'm not sure why the order matters, but I guess hierarchy is important in something like this, and Oliver is always grateful for the opportunity to be alone with his girl while the rest of us are just glad we don't have to witness them pawing at each other for ten fucking minutes.

Sooner than I think any of us anticipated, we're pulling into the Pendleton Prep grounds, making our way through the quiet campus and down the driveway to the house. After pulling the tie off my neck, I shove it in a pocket as the three of us climb out of the car and wearily head up the stairs, when the front door opens ahead of us.

"Gentlemen, can we have five minutes of your time?" a lady asks, her black mask unfamiliar, though the voice I've heard before.

This is the woman who looks after the Angels. Lisa? Liza? No, Liselle.

Nodding, I push past, following her outstretched hand as my stomach twists, regretting putting Ivy in that other car, because if The Sect is here, then what the hell has or is about to happen?

An open bottle of champagne chills on ice in the middle of the table, the girls sitting nervously as Ivy's panicked gaze meets mine. At least she's here, safe, even if *we* may not be for much longer.

Liselle follows us in, taking the seat beside the masked man at the head of the table, the champagne flute looking tiny in his hands.

"Fantastic! Here you are!" the man booms. "The final three."

Wait. What?

"Grab yourselves a glass, gentlemen. It's time to celebrate," Liselle says, gesturing excitedly to the filled glasses on the table.

"Unfortunately, it would appear Miss Coombs raised the lowest amount of money at your fundraiser," the man explains. "Meaning her and Mr James have been removed from the competition."

Shit. *This* was a challenge, but not for us.

They made the finale about the Angels without telling us *or* them.

Blindly, I reach for a glass, sitting heavily in the closest seat as the words attempt to penetrate

This is it.

We made it.

"There will be an official ceremony at the end of the week," Liselle continues. "But we didn't want to wait to give you the good news."

Good news for us. Not so much for Oliver and Stephanie.

Liselle says more words, her red-masked partner raising a toast that we all join them in numbly. We're going through the motions on nothing more than autopilot at this point, smiling, nodding, doing all the things we're supposed to.

They toast, we cheer, nothing sinking in as we wish then goodnight and they congratulation us once again, locking the door behind them before we make our way upstairs, closing ourselves away in the relative safety of our room.

"So, that's it?" I confirm for what feels like the millionth time as we all drop into the sectional, with Ivy cuddling up beside Wyatt, his arm draping around her back.

"Looks like it." Leo shrugs, running his hand through his hair, then leaning his elbows against his knees. "It kind of makes sense, though."

"How's that?"

"There was no way they'd have let Oliver through, and his biggest weakness was the crazy bitch he tied himself to."

"She wasn't that bad," Ivy argues, but there's next to no strength behind it. Stephanie has been demeaning and belittling to anyone and everyone for months, but no more, I guess.

"But Stephanie wouldn't have been able to convince anyone outside of her circle that those items were worth bartering for. She doesn't... or didn't have the ability to charm anyone, ever," Leo argues.

"You talked up more than just yours with the potential

investors. You got to know their likes and interests and made sure to find the right things for everyone, whereas, from what I heard, Stephanie spent the night chatting with her friends, hoping that was going to be enough," Wyatt says placing a kiss on the top of Ivy's head.

"And you and Penelope did most of the actual organising," Leo adds, tapping his finger against his lip in thought.

"So, after sorting through our physical, emotional, and mental strengths, our teamwork and problem-solving abilities, and how well we can follow rules, the final test was for the women that are going to stand by us. An opportunity for them to showcase their abilities, to take a short timescale and a half-cocked idea and turn it into something classy and fortuitous," Wyatt says, looking at the bigger picture.

"Yeah, I'd have never figured that would be their plan," I admit, thinking of all the weird and wonderful ideas we came up with whilst brainstorming. None of which involved the Angels.

"That's it, then," Ivy repeats, catching Leo's gaze before her green eyes come to me, excitement and something else swirling through their depths. "You're safe." She jumps up, crossing the room as she climbs onto Leo's lap, pushing him back against the sofa before taking his face in her hands. "You're free," she says.

"Oh, angel. We'll never be free," Leo counters on an exhale, his realism such a contrast to the cup-half-full that she pours from.

He's right. The Sect is always going to have things it wants from us. They're not just setting us up for life and handing us power without expecting something in return. Even I'm not that naïve.

"But you're in. Your places are secure. No more challenges. No more fighting. No more looking over your shoulder or waiting for the other shoe to drop. This is it. You made it," Ivy says.

Her excitement trickles through the room, dripping slowly from one man to the next as the truth of her words sinks in.

"We're in. Now we can find Jacob."

Leo's gaze flies to mine, his hands stalling their glide up the inside of Ivy's blouse as thoughts of rescue and vengeance flicker across his face before a smile eventually forms.

"Now we can find Jacob," he agrees, pulling Ivy farther down into his lap and nuzzling against her chest as she languishes in his hold.

The energy in the room shifts. No longer are we lavishing in the what's-been, now we're looking ahead to the what's-coming. To the future that finally feels attainable.

To my side, Wyatt pops the top two buttons on his shirt, shucking his shoes before closing the distance to them and pressing up against Ivy's back as her head tips against his stomach, looking up at him with stars in her eyes.

There is so much love in the look he gives her that it hurts. It holds me in place on the sofa, able to do nothing more than watch their lust unfold.

It's not the first time I've found myself an observer to the three of them. Last time, I had my brother at my side getting just as turned on by them as I was. Now, though, we're holding together, waiting for the moment the space he's supposed to be in is filled once again.

By the time my brain switches back on to what's happening right in front of me, Ivy's blouse is hanging off her shoulders, the cups of her bra shoved out of the way as Leo licks and lathes her perfect nipple whilst Wyatt plunges his tongue in her mouth, and she writhes between the two of them.

"You wet, angel?" Leo asks, looking up at her under his heavy lids.

"So wet," she confirms on a nod.

"You joining us?" Leo asks, turning his head to pin me with a look.

His traitorous tongue flicks her pebbled nipple as she shudders in Wyatt's grip, the three of them something out of a wet dream.

"Get her clothes off and I'll think about it," I counter, my dick not getting the memo as it presses against the front of my dress pants.

Leo raises an eyebrow as he clocks the twitch in my pants before smirking and shoving her shirt off. Wyatt helps Ivy up and out of her trousers and thong whilst Leo gets rid of his clothes. Within nothing more than a minute they're all hot, naked, and needy.

Ivy seats herself back over Leo's lap as Wyatt holds her tits, offering them up to Leo. She arches into the touch as he moves from one to the other, grinding against his length. I can almost imagine the way she'd feel in my hands, the way her body would glide against my thighs as she moans.

They barley notice me move as I slide away to the bed

to grab a bottle of lube from the side table before coming back to the sofa and undoing my pants. Sitting back where I was gives me the perfect view of them winding her up, her breathy moans and whines heating the room to a fever pitch.

"What was the verdict, then? Is she wet?" I ask, knowing full well she will be.

Leo nods as Wyatt's hand glides down, sliding through her slick folds as she bucks against him, clearly close.

"Are you going to take them both?" I ask, gesturing to the lube I dropped beside them.

Her excited gaze flicks to mine as she runs her tongue quickly along her bottom lip before pressing them together, a moment of nervous anticipation wracking over her.

"Have you ever done that before?" Leo asks, adjusting her in his lap as Wyatt presses against her clit, pushing and pulling her against Leo's length; a tease that I love and hate in equal measure.

She grinds against the two of them, crashing her lips against Leo's as he swallows the scream I know she'd have let fly as she comes undone in their arms. Wyatt shuffles, and Leo's hips buck, sliding her down his length.

Ivy's responsive moan has me almost coming on the spot, her head dropping back against Wyatt as he presses his length against her lower back.

"Do you fancy that, angel?" Leo asks again as Wyatt lubes up his fingers, playing with her arse whilst Leo thrusts lazily in and out of her pussy, and my own hand finally comes to my aching cock.

It's nowhere near the velvet warmth of her pussy, but she chose them for this moment. I'll wait. Ivy rocks and rolls between them, her lips going back to Leo's as they work her higher and higher.

"He's going to need the words, sugar. Are you going to take them both like a good girl? Let them make you feel so good," I tell her, trying my best to not think of the fullness and the tightness they're about to experience.

"Yes. God, yes," she pants.

Leo adjusts again, moving Ivy so that Wyatt has better access. She cries out as Wyatt groans, the tip of his dick disappearing as her body adjusts.

"Just breathe," Leo explains. "I promise it'll feel so good."

They wait until she relaxes between them again, her body going soft and pliable as Wyatt continues, the restraint showing on his face when he finally gets seated, dragging out slowly before pushing back in as the two of them find a rhythm.

"You good?" Wyatt asks, checking in with Ivy, even as she moans and writhes in ecstasy.

"I need him," she replies breathlessly, gesturing wildly in my direction "I need all of you."

Not one to deny a wet, begging woman asking for me, my shirt hits the floor seconds later as I take the three steps over to them. Ivy's hand reaches out for me as I step on the sofa beside them, my hard dick bobbing just above Leo's eye level.

"You can keep your tongue to your fucking self," I growl out as Leo smirks, dropping his head back against the cushions, holding Ivy in place while she wraps her lips around me.

Fuck, she feels good, and barely moments later, I can feel that telltale tingle at the bottom of my spine.

"Come for me, Ivy," I demand, wrapping her hair around my fist, doing my best to stave off the impending explosion, even as we all hold on for her.

The boys pick up their pace, and one of them must rub her clit, because seconds later, she's swallowing my dick down as she quakes between us, dragging Leo along with her. Wyatt pulls out, spraying over her perfect arse as I unload down her throat.

Spent, she collapses into Leo's chest.

Tucking myself away, I head to the bathroom and run a cloth under the warm water before helping to clean her up. Leo drops his T-shirt over her body as she curls into his side completely boneless. And for the first time in a long time, the four of us climb into bed together, ready for whatever comes next.

NINE

Ivy

The lyrics of "Love Gone Blind" blast through my earphones while I concentrate on putting one foot in front of the other, pounding down the gravel driveway in time to neither my heartbeat nor the music in my head as the house finally comes back into view. But instead of going to the entrance, I circle around, following the path to the pool house and the place this entire venture began.

I had no intention of ever coming back here, but for some reason, I find myself drawn to the tiny, tucked away space I briefly called home… back when I was learning to live with a whole bunch of new people, resenting the fact I even had to be here. I guess, in some ways, not much has changed, and in others, life is completely different.

After sliding my key in, I push open the front door, the house silent as I make my way down the corridor and into the kitchen and living room. There's a stray mug still on the coffee table, and a dish towel left out on the side. Surprising, I suppose, that the cleaners haven't been back since the girls decided to move into the main house.

Interesting, too, that there was never any comeback on that.

I hover in the kitchen, my gaze flicking to what used to be mine and Tamsin's room as I remember the crushing heartbreak of walking through the glass doors to nothing but silence. Like this but not. This is a silence created by the lack of sound in a space that's empty, vacant, alone. Not one that's supposed to be filled with love and laughter. Not now, anyway.

Turning up that day to find the room half empty and my best friend gone was the beginning of the end for the pool house. Within nothing more than a few weeks, we had all begun to take this more seriously, to pair up, back ourselves up, and find comfort wherever it could be found.

Life here was simple, easy, in comparison, but all that is done now. It's over. Complete.

The boys made it to the final three.

The only thing remaining is to find a way to get Jacob back in our clutches, and I'm hoping, now that we're at the end, the way to do that will become clearer.

Making my way across the room, my fingers trail along the bedroom door before I reach for the handle, my hand hovering over it before turning away and heading for the coffee cup and back to the kitchen. Dumping out the mouldy remnants of someone's tea, I wash it up and put away the towel, stalling.

I don't know why I came here, but as I stand in the middle of the kitchen in the house we made a home, I still can't make myself open that bedroom door.

Everything I had in there is gone. The girls and Wyatt brought it all over to the main house months ago, and there aren't even scrap remnants of my friend in there anymore. No, The Sect is far too efficient for that.

Maybe I just came to remind myself that she *was* here.

That she existed. Or maybe I needed to remember where we came from to appreciate where we're going to go, and the doors that The Sect are going to be able to open. I don't know.

Whatever it was, I'm not sure I find it as my phone buzzes in its strap on my arm. With a sigh, I head back out, locking the door and making my way through the garden and around the pool before letting myself into the main house.

Laughter peels from the den as I reach for a bottle of water from the fridge, Aimee clearly finding whatever she's watching amusing. The door to the gym is open as I pass; the guys probably still working out down there.

Bypassing it, I head into the den, joining Aimee as the sweat on my brow begins to cool.

"Mind if I join you?"

"Of course not," she replies with a smile.

It's like all the weight of the last few months has evaporated from her shoulders. She moved in here, almost paired up with Jasper before he was *removed*, then watched her best friend get murdered in cold blood.

An unvoluntary shiver ripples down my spine when I think back to the events of New Year's Eve, and the way that's shaped the last month. Hearing that someone is willing to kill for what they believe in is nowhere near the same as seeing it happen.

That, coupled with the cold and detached way Thomas and his wife moved on with the evening like it didn't even happen left us all in a state of shock. Shock that seems to have worn off now we are through to the final six.

"No Penelope?" I ask, sinking into one of the sofas.

"No, she had to go out and meet a friend, but she promised to bring back some of that chocolate cake we both like."

"I'm not going to say no to cake," I agree as my phone vibrates again.

Going back to her programme, I slide it from the strap on my arm and open it up, expecting something from the guys or the group chat. Instead, it's Ruby.

Ruby: *Heard the fundraiser went well.*

Ruby: *Thought I'd have heard from you about it, but that's cool.*

Things have been slowly but surely getting easier between us. The conversations are a little less stilted, and the communication is going both ways of its own accord. She can still be off-hand and quite guarded sometimes, but effort is being made by both of us now, which makes it feel one hell of a lot easier.

Me: *Sorry I didn't let you know last night. Things got complicated. We're still waiting to hear the final numbers.*

Complicated… always.

When the news eventually sank in that we're finally safe, I couldn't believe the amount of relief I felt. I honestly hadn't realised how much tension I'd been holding over the whole thing until it was gone.

The chefs are almost silent as they pass the entrance to the den, heading to the dining room to set up.

"Oops. I didn't realise it was this late. I'm going to warn the guys and jump in the shower. See you at dinner," I explain, flying another text off and shoving my phone back in its holder before heading upstairs.

Thirty minutes later, I'm mulling over a reply from Ruby, clean and changed, when Wyatt joins me on the sectional in our suite while Nick and Leo are getting changed.

"Penny for your thoughts," Wyatt says, sitting beside me before pulling me into his side and wrapping me in his comforting embrace.

"Ruby is complaining again," I gripe.

I can't exactly explain why in here. No doubt The Sect is still listening, but this isn't the first time she's messaged me to get Leo off her back.

Of course, he wants answers, movement, something. We all do. But he's becoming obsessive with it to the wrong person. I'm sure if she could do something more than go between, she would, but it's a tricky balance.

"I'll talk to him," Wyatt offers while I fly a response off to her. "When will you be seeing the Little Sisters again, or is your obligation complete now the fundraiser is done?"

"Good question. I don't know."

I'm not sure I'd call them an obligation anymore. Sure, at the beginning it was something we were ordered to do, but spending time with the Little Sisters has become more than something we *have* to do. We haven't had more than twice-monthly briefs or a refresher training session in ages, choosing to meet up with the girls individually in our own time rather than en-masse. To be honest, it was getting harder to explain the sadness and the missing people as the weeks passed. It just seemed easier to avoid the discussions completely. But now that we're a final six, there'll be no more people leaving, and it would be nice to get them all together again.

"I'll have a chat with Aimee and Penelope and see if they want to do something altogether. I'm sure there will be a final hurrah at some point, but I'd like to keep in touch with Ruby, and I'm sure they will, too."

"What was that? You've heard from Ruby?" Nick asks as the walk-in wardrobe door opens behind us.

"Ruby? Of course, she can text you but not me," Leo grumbles, checking his phone for probably the millionth time today.

"I was just talking about meeting up with all the Little Sisters now we're at the end," I explain, the hope draining from both their faces. "Sorry."

"No, I'm sorry. I jumped the gun," Nick counters, holding his hands out to pull me up from the sofa. "Let's go get some food. I'm starving."

The four of us make our way downstairs, the empty room beside ours a reminder that getting here hasn't been without sacrifice as we meet Aimee in the entranceway.

"Is Penelope not back?" I ask, peering around the doorway to the den.

"No, but I thought she would have been by now, and her phone is going straight to voicemail," Aimee replies, concern showing in her gaze as she looks longingly at the front door, clearly hoping it's going to open, and Penelope's going to waltz in any second.

But she doesn't... and so, with a disappointed sigh, Aimee follows us through to the dining room, stopping dead behind the guys as we take in the thick envelope on the table and the dress boxes laid out... again.

Shit. What now?

"Should we wait for Pen?" Aimee asks nervously as the five of us find the boxes with our names on and spread out around the table unconsciously.

"Definitely," Leo says, pulling out his chair and sitting as he eyes the boxes like whatever nightmare they have in store for us might jump out of them. He grabs the envelope and pulls the card out. "Congratulations to the you, the Pendleton Prep finalists. Your induction ceremony will commence at nine p.m. on Friday. Please be ready for collection thirty minutes prior."

"Well, at least they're being polite this time," Aimee says with a cringe, stroking her fingers along the embossing. "That's progress, right?"

I nod as her worried gaze flicks to mine, and we fall into silence, the minutes ticking by slowly as we all try Penelope's phone again, but to no avail. After twenty minutes, the chef tells us to go ahead and open the boxes. "Penelope's can be sequestered to her room."

Leaving, he takes her box, looking just as confused as we are.

"She's not gone-gone, right?" I ask once he's out of the room.

"All of her stuff is upstairs. She literally just went out for coffee," Aimee says as she pulls the lid off, peeling back the paper. "And there is a box with her name on it right there. She's not gone-gone."

Pushing down the hesitation, I open mine too, pulling out a full-length white robe similar to the black ones the guys have; the kind everyone else wore when we were 'unveiled' to The Sect way back when.

"I guess this is really it, then," Nick says, pulling the mask out of the bottom of his box. "It's official."

His words don't hold any of the excitement I thought getting to the end of this thing would elicit. Of course, that's because there's still a part of him missing: Jacob. But maybe this end will hold answers and be a way to get Jacob out and back with us. Time will tell.

"It looks like it," Aimee agrees with a small smile.

The boxes are put to one side with the card, and dinner is served, the meal passing by in a blur of food and nerves as we talk about meeting up with the Little sisters and speculate as to what might happen Friday night.

It's been something of a relaxing Sunday off, which is not something any of us usually manage to enjoy, but the weight of everything finally feels to be lifting, if only in time for Penelope to go missing and leave more questions hanging over our heads.

At the end of the meal, Wyatt and Leo take Aimee and drive to the coffee shop, but there's no sign of Penelope or her car. Nobody even remembers her going in there, which should be more of a concern than the fact that the owner came down three hours after closing to talk to them.

It's like she went out for coffee and just disappeared, except that the robe came for her and all of her clothes are still in the wardrobe, as well as her books on the shelf. So, it's not down to The Sect. Something weird is going on.

Penelope doesn't show up on Monday or Tuesday, and there are no further words from The Sect about it either. By the time Wednesday lunchtime rolls around, we are all a little on edge. Things have never gone unexplained like this before. Since we're about to hit the end of this stupid game, this feels like a huge hiccup.

I'm just about to call Wyatt, looking for my ride, when Aimee pulls up, the campus busy around us as students rush from one place to the next, doing their best to stay out of the spring showers the beautiful English weather is gracing us with.

"Hey, girl. Are you free to give me a hand with an assignment? I thought I had what I needed, but I'm one survey short," Aimee asks as she shoves through the glass doors, keeping out the worst of the weather.

"Well, Wyatt isn't here, so I guess I can spare some time," I reply, sending him a quick message as I take one last look outside.

I really wanted to get back and work on my own assignment—the one due any day now—but the message stays unread, and concern builds in my stomach. He always replies.

"You're saving my arse. Do you have time now? I've got everything with me..." Aimee prompts, drawing my attention back to her pleading face and away from the phone in my hand.

"Sure." I shrug with a sigh, slinging my bag over my shoulder and following her to the library. I'm going to get soaked walking down that driveway. I may as well kill half an hour here with her whilst I wait for Wyatt to come back to me.

I check my phone intermittently, answering her questions distractedly as I attempt to work out what would make Wyatt late and mean he doesn't pick up a message, throwing one in the group chat, too. But the only times this has happened before has been when they've been in challenges, and that's not the case now… is it?

It's forty-five minutes later when I make it back to the glass doors at the front of the building, and there is still no sign of Wyatt and no response from him or the group chat. That's when I know deep in my bones that something is going on.

Leaving Aimee tucked safely in the back of the library, I throw my hood over my head and push out into the awful weather, doing my best to make my way down the driveway quickly on foot.

The old stone house looks ominous in the half-light as the rain pours, much like it did on the first day we arrived here, when Tamsin and I drove down the secluded street full of excitement, and trepidation. I guess some things never change. Lights shine on the ground floor, but nothing about them feels friendly as I push my key into the lock, go in, and close the door loudly behind me before I turn to lock it.

"Well, it's about time someone got here," someone calls from behind me, their voice broken and scratchy, but something I feared I'd never hear again. I'm sure my heart has stopped, and I've gone into some kind of hallucination from the rain soaking through my clothes, but as my heartbeat thunders in my ears, drowning out everything else, I'm reminded that it hasn't.

My bag drops to the floor beside me before I dare turn around, not ready to know I've completely lost it, and my paranoia has turned into physical figments of my imagination. Except when I do, he's really there.

"Jacob…"

TEN

Nick

The two taps on the door echo around the silent hall, but nobody is paying it any attention as we concentrate on the problems on the page and getting to the end of them before the class ends. Then the door opens, and my name is called, making my blood turn to ice.

"If you could follow me, please," the man says, his shuttered gaze catching mine.

I have no idea who he is or what he wants, but if he's turning up halfway through an exam and pulling me out of class, it's not good news.

"You can make it up at a later date," the professor promises, looking fearfully from his tablet to the man at the door and then to me.

With a nod, I close everything up and pack it away in my bag, doing my best not to run through every worst-case scenario until we're out of the building and I'm climbing into the back of a blacked-out SUV.

This screams The Sect, and when we pull into the old church car park not fifteen minutes later, it couldn't be anyone else. Leo's car pulls up beside us, Leo and Wyatt climbing out as the concern in my stomach builds.

I thought this was all over. I thought we were done.

They share my look of apprehension as the three of us walk up the steps, pressing through the heavy wooden door into an empty room. Except there were also two other vehicles outside, meaning we're definitely not alone in here.

The chief of police steps out from a side door, apologising for keeping us as he pulls a couple of chairs together by the altar, and the four of us sit down awkwardly.

Maybe this is just another opportunity for him to congratulate us… like Lisa what's-her-name did the other night?

"Sorry about pulling you out early today. We would usually complete this as part of the ceremony on Friday night, but due to a few moving parts, we've moved it up," he says cryptically.

"Okay," Wyatt says.

None of us have any idea about what happens as part of this ceremony. And, whilst both Leo and Wyatt's fathers are here to ask, neither of them are handing any information over about it. So, we're still in the dark, but whatever he's *bringing forward* can't be good.

"You all took an oath back at the beginning of the initiations, but do you remember the wording of that oath?" the chief of police asks. "Specifically, about leaving."

Leaving? This has got to do with Penelope being missing.

"Not exactly," I admit.

"Let me refresh your memory. There is no way out from here except by death or excommunication." The chief of police looks at each of us, searching our gazes for something before continuing. "When each of your fellow initiates have been removed from the competition, they have been offered the opportunity to continue their promise to The Sect, albeit in a difference capacity to how they intended it to be."

This is what Wyatt's contact had said: servitude.

"Some chose to continue their work with us, some didn't. Now, those who no longer wish to honour their oaths have made their decision, and we all know what that means, right? That means the only way left is…" He pauses, apparently waiting for one of us to fill in the missing blank before he finishes with, "Death."

The word hangs in the air like a shotgun going off in the quiet.

"And part of the ritual of acceptance to The Sect is a blood sacrifice. The blood of those who were not worthy," he continues.

I'm waiting for him to crack a smile, to laugh and tell us this is all just a joke, but the silence lingers until the side door opens again, with three bodies being hauled through as we all stand, and the chairs are moved and lined up.

George, Stephanie, and Oliver are unceremoniously dumped in the chairs in front of Wyatt, Leo and I, three guns being placed on the final one. They're already beaten and bloody, Stephanie's top half hanging off her shoulder, their hands cuffed behind them as anger radiates from the three of them.

"You have got to be fucking kidding me," George grumbles loudly, the words muffled and smearing together with his busted-up face.

George glowers at Wyatt, and Oliver sneers at me, likely thinking none of us will be able to do this. But we have to, don't we?

"Guns are locked and loaded when you're ready gentlemen," the chief of police says as he steps back, out of our line of sight, but close enough to step in if needed.

The guys that hauled them in have disappeared, and Leo hands me a gun, weighing the one in his hand. It's suddenly clear he's got the hardest one here…

Stephanie.

ELEVEN

Wyatt

I'm the quiet one: thoughtful, loyal, calculated.

There isn't any of the barely restrained danger lurking behind Leo's eyes hidden in my veins. Not a drop.

Leo doesn't even blink when he pulls the trigger, finally silencing the woman that has bitched and manipulated her way through the last half a dozen months. The same one who swore he wouldn't have the nerve to do it just seconds ago. I guess that didn't work out so well for her.

There's a sort of cold silence that falls over me—a blanket of apathy almost—but it doesn't cover the rest of the room, because I can still see Oliver's mouth moving, the vein in his neck throbbing wildly as he hurls insults at Nick whilst I studiously avoid the man, his words, and the machinery right beside me. The life I'm supposed to be ending.

Nick paces, and words are said, not that any of them grace my ears, because I'm trapped in some kind of stunned bubble as the seconds unfold before me. Nick steps closer to Oliver, pressing the gun beneath his chin before turning away again, his pacing beginning anew as he shakes his head and wrings his hands.

Some small part of me knows I should be doing the same. Trying. Attempting. Working my way out of the fractured moment I've found myself in and back to the task at hand. After all, we knew that blood would be a stipulation eventually, didn't we?

The Sect will need something to hold over our heads. To keep us in line.

Before I realise it's happening, the gun goes off, and Oliver crumples in the chair.

It's like I'm watching the whole thing from outside my body, floating somewhere in the rafters of the abandoned building as both Nick and Leo turn to me, worry crossing their beautiful faces. Leo takes a step closer, but he's told to stop before he even moves, the singular word breaking the mental barrier that's been erected around me.

"No assistance needed," we're told.

Why this one is being witnessed, I don't know. Why the three of us are in this room together and not in individual pods, I don't know, either.

Everything up until this point has been singular, us against each other or the clock, except for maybe the early challenges. But even the escape rooms dwindled to one-on-one eventually. Yet here we are, the three 'victors,' slaying our final demons together.

Letting George's vicious words sink through the armour I've erected, I finally admit their truth.

I am nothing.

Not worthy of the place I've been given.

Of The Sect.

Of Nick, Leo, Jacob, and Ivy.

I shouldn't be the one wielding his demise.

After all, I'm just the quiet one. The one making sure all the people are where they're supposed to be, ensuring we all make it through the best we can.

No, I wasn't the one handing out drugs to beautiful young women. I wasn't the one drinking too much, fucking too much, mouthing off too much. That was him. I was the one planning and prepping for this very moment. The one where I stake my claim in The Sect and take my birthright in both hands.

The gun is heavier than I anticipate, or maybe that's just the weight of expectation as I point and squeeze, closing my eyes as the recoil jars my arm backwards. And then someone is prying the gun from my fingers, and someone else is wrapping me in their arms, pressing my face into their chest.

If the broad shoulders are anything to go by, it's Nick, and if the rustling of clothing is anything to go by, Leo is cleaning the weapons of prints. Not that I imagine that will do us any good now.

The three of us are dismissed, and Leo collects the jacket he discarded before shooting our former friend as we head out. I follow, nothing but the sound of our steps echoing around the ancient building, the concrete, and eventually the stairs and gravel until we're standing beside a car. Leo's car.

"I need your shirt," Leo says, wiping the inside of his across my face before handing it to Nick and asking for his hoodie.

God only knows what is spattered all over me. Something warm, now tacky. Blood. Life force. Something George no longer has or needs.

Leo helps me take off my shirt, then slides his jacket over my shoulders before telling us both to get in the car. I'm not going to ask why he has plastic bags in his boot, or what he's going to do with the now blood-spattered clothes—burn them probably. After all, he was the one who took charge after Oliver nearly beat someone to death. At least he won't be doing that again.

We climb in the car, and Leo turns the engine over before peeling out of the car park, making gravel fly everywhere as if he can out drive the demons he just let loose.

"I've never… have you ever done that before?" I ask, staring vacantly out of the back passenger window.

"No," Nick admits in front of me.

Leo is surprisingly quiet until he confesses, "Yes," on an exhale.

The car falls quiet as we make our way back through the gates of Pendleton Prep, a hollowness in my bones that wasn't there before. Is this what taking a life does to a person? Scoops out your insides and leaves you nothing but a shell of the person you used to be? Because no amount of telling myself it was him or me, them or us, will change the fact that I knowingly pulled that trigger.

No doubt The Sect would have killed us alongside them if we'd refused. God, I can only imagine the shit show that would have devolved into as we pull past the residential buildings, with flashing blue lights surrounding the entrance of the main administration building.

"Are those police vans or ambulances?" I ask, attempting to peer through the torrent of rain as I press between the seats.

"Both," Leo replies as he pulls over, shouting out of the window to the closest student he can find. "Yo! What's going on?" he asks.

"It looks like a student was stabbed. I don't know if they're alive, but the paramedics haven't made it out yet," the student explains, sheltering behind the car from the worst of the wind.

"Should we—" I start.

"There's nothing we can do right now," Leo cuts me off before going back to the person shivering beside of him. "Keep me in the loop, yeah?"

The student nods, shaking Leo's hand before going back to the huddle of people at the side of the building.

"We're half-dressed and covered in blood. There's no way any of us are walking into an active crime scene right now," Leo explains, setting back off and heading for the driveway and the safety of home.

Home… what a weird word to use for this place.

We've been watched, listened to, observed, and monitored whilst The Sect have pressed rules and restrictions on us, forced us through challenges and obstacles whilst trying to build friendships, relationships, and keep ourselves sane. I hope they've been enjoying the show, because once we're officially sworn in, this has got to be over, surely?

The rain pours harder as we move quickly between the trees, the darkness wrapping around the car like the feeling in the pit of my stomach: tumultuous.

That's got to be it now, though, right? We're through to the final three, all the competition has been removed, and they no doubt have plenty of blackmail material to use against us. Once we're officially fully fledged members, there'll be no more need for these dramatics.

"What do you think that was all about?" Nick asks, gesturing back at the campus while we wait for the garage doors to slide open.

"Nothing good," Leo replies ominously.

"At least it's nothing to do with us this time," I say, pulling Leo's jacket around my shoulders.

"Let's hope not," Nick replies.

TWELVE

Ivy

"**W**hat? How? When? Oh. My. God."

The questions tumble from me without thought as I dive across the open space and wrap my arms and legs around him, leaping into his open embrace.

Jacob chuckles beneath me as he adjusts his hold on me, not ready to let me go either as he snuggles in closer, the two of us standing the entranceway completely lost to everything else going on around us.

"Where is everyone?" he asks, eventually peeling back and placing me back on the floor.

"Aimee's in the library, Penelope is MIA, and the guys are… well, I don't actually know where they are." I huff out an unimpressed laugh as I pull my phone from my pocket, checking it again, but there's still no reply.

"And the rest of them?" he asks, because he's been away since New Year's Eve, and he has no idea all of the shit that's gone on in the last month.

"Oh… erm. Charlotte didn't make it through the New Year thing…" *Dead.* "And Oliver and Stephanie went out during the last challenge." *Also, probably dead.* "We've made it through to the final six! Or seven, I suppose if you're here… but then Penelope is unaccounted for, so at this point I really have no idea how many of us are left," I ramble.

"Woah. I've missed a lot," he replies, rubbing his hand across his five o'clock shadow.

The action draws my attention to his face, making me really look at him and take in the changes over the last few weeks. His eyes are sunken, with deep circles lining them, and his clothes hang differently. He's thinner, gaunt almost, and his eyes are haunted.

Whatever he's been going through with The Sect hasn't been sunshine and rainbows, that's for sure.

"Let's get you something to eat and I'll fill you in. Hopefully the guys will be back soon and then you can tell us what you've been up to. It'll be easier to just go through it once, I imagine."

"God, yes." The relief that tumbles from him is palpable, and whether that's because this buys him some more time to figure out the words or because he's really that interested in whatever I can rustle up in the kitchen, I'm not sure. "I forgot how good the food here is," he comments, the smell of fresh pizza still lingering in the air from lunch.

"The menu is on the wall, and the chefs should be here shortly," I say, filling the coffee machine before finding us some mugs and grabbing the last couple of brownies from the cupboard, needing something to do rather than stand here and gawp at him.

"Whatever it is will be better than…" His sentence trails off with a shudder, his concentration a million miles away.

"I'm sure it'll be practically orgasmic."

His eyes light up when I scoop two healthy servings of ice cream over the warmed brownies and hand one over, along with a steaming mug of coffee.

"Just what the doctor ordered on a cold and wet winter, or spring, I suppose, afternoon," I say with a nod.

"I'm not going to argue with that. Now, tell me everything I've missed," Jacob asks, fork in hand.

We spend the next forty minutes sitting at the kitchen counter whilst I fill him in on everything. The rest of the New Year's party, Aimee pulling away from the group, Oliver doing his best to wind Nick up and push his way between the guys, all the way through to the fundraising and the twist that turned out to be. Not least of all for Oliver and Stephanie.

"And they've managed to hold it together, Leo and Nick? They've not beaten each other senseless?"

"There have been moments, and the strain is showing in all of us, not just the two of them." If anyone was ever unsure as to how vital each part of our unit is, this has certainly shown it. "They're going to be so overwhelmed when they get back from wherever the hell they are."

"You don't know?" he asks with the cock of his head.

But before I have chance to reply, the entrance door bangs closed, and their hushed voices carry through to the kitchen. Jacob pauses, his cup halfway to his mouth as I call out for Nick.

"Before you go any further, give me those shoes," Leo clips out. "Both of you."

Grumbling, Nick must do what he's asked before

coming through, stopping dead in the doorway, forcing Wyatt to walk straight into the back of him, an oomph tumbling from his lips.

It takes the longest of seconds for it to register on Nick's face that Jacob is sitting right here. Now. In real life. You can almost see the argument his brain is having with his heart as to whether or not he's currently taking a break from reality, but the moment reality registers, he strides across the room and wraps his brother in his arms.

Wyatt calls for Leo, telling him to abandon whatever he was about to do, and the relief on his face when he walks in to find Jacob and Nick both here is immeasurable. Leo gives the two of them time to break apart before shoving Nick out of the way and crashing his lips against Jacob's.

So much is said in that kiss. There's an entire conversation happening as the three of us wait them out. Although you can see how it physically pains Nick to do it, and how eager Wyatt is to share his excitement, they both mange to hang back… for a minute or two at least.

All too soon, the excitement builds, and questions are being asked over the top of each other as everyone argues for answers, wherever the hell they've been and what on earth they've been doing now completely forgotten.

"What's that on your face?" I ask, gesturing to a dirty mark on the edge of Wyatt's cheek. "And where's your shirt?"

The whole room goes silent, and suddenly, I realise that Jacob and I have missed something important. Wyatt shudders, declaring he needs to shower before walking out. Leo looks at the plastic bag in his hands, with half their clothes and shoes inside it.

"I'd better…" Leo trails off, stepping away. "Nick can fill you in, I'm sure."

Findlay and Matthew, the two chefs, arrive, and as Leo slides out of the back door, Nick, Jacob, and I are ushered out of the kitchen.

"Your robes are hanging in the wardrobe, Mr Barrett," Findlay comments, looking at Jacob briefly before following his colleague into the kitchen.

"I guess that means you're back for good, then?" Nick asks hopefully as we make our way up the stairs and along the corridor, heading back to our suite.

Jacob answers with a silent nod, and when we take in the white robes hanging beside mine, his clothing and shoes all lined back up, it's clear he's here to stay.

"Where the hell have you lot been?" I ask as Wyatt drops onto the sofa, pulling me into his lap, despite the water dripping from the ends of his hair. "You were supposed to pick me up."

"I know. I'm sorry. The Sect needed us to do something ahead of the ceremony on Friday," Wyatt explains.

"Yeah, take out the rubbish," Nick grumbles.

"What?" I ask, my confusion clear.

"It doesn't matter. It's done now," Wyatt says with a heavy sigh.

It takes another half an hour for Leo to join us, the smell of smoke hanging from him when he comes back in the room and nods our way before heading straight to the shower, with Jacob soon following him.

"I take it your 'taking out the rubbish' had something to

do with whatever he's been burning," I say.

"Yeah, not that it would do us any good, anyway," Nick replies despondently.

We fall into silence, something playing on the TV that none of us are paying attention to.

"It's probably all linked," Jacob says, coming back into the room with Leo hot on his tail. "Someone is missing, aren't they? One of the girls," he calls, breaking us out of the reverie we've found ourselves in.

"Yeah. We can't find Penelope," I tell him, looking over my shoulder.

The weariness still sits behind his eyes, but there's something else there now, too. Acceptance or understanding. He finally feels like he's home… safe. Or he's starting to.

"It's not been for lack of trying, either. The guys went to the coffee place she was supposed to be meeting her friend at, but she never turned up. We've tried calling her family, but the butler just keeps hanging up."

Stephanie was Penelope's best friend, and now that she's failed the final challenge and gone too, we have no idea where to even start looking for poor Penelope.

"I guess because The Sect can't find her, they've put me back in her place," Jacob deduces. "I'm a bloodline member, so I get allowances the others don't, apparently. And because they require six finalists, and one is currently unavailable, I guess… here I am," Jacob says.

Leo dops into the corner of the sectional, pulling Jacob in between his legs and pressing Jacob's back to his chest, not ready to let him go just yet.

"So, you got a way in," Leo ponders over his shoulder.

"And because she's missing, The Sect needed to get something on us quicker than usual and moved the blood sacrifice up. Now, the only players on the board are blood members and those willing to stand by the oaths they took," Wyatt says, putting all the pieces together.

"I'm sorry, what? Blood sacrifices?" I ask, thinking of the dried glob of whatever that was on him. "Actually, don't tell me. I don't want to know." I'm just grateful I didn't have to partake in that particular endeavour. Gross.

"Trust me, you don't," Nick comments with a shudder.

Leo pulls his phone out, concern flickering over his features before he types out some kind of message. "Shit. Where's Aimee?"

"I left her in the library earlier on, why?"

"Then, she should be back by now?" he asks, not looking up from the conversation he's having on his phone.

"I dunno. I guess so. She was typing up my interview and adjusting her notes before starting on the main body of her assignment," I explain. "But then I came home to Jacob, and then you all turned up and I completely forgot about it. I can go and check her room, though, if you need her for something."

"Sorry, chick. She's not there. She didn't make it," Leo replies, looking up from his phone.

Didn't make it from what?

"That's who…" Wyatt says, his arms tightening around me.

Leo nods, the two of them having a conversation I'm not privy to.

"There were police and ambulances on campus when we

got back. Someone had been stabbed," Nick explains. "We just needed to get back and get cleaned up after everything that happened at the church, so we didn't go and investigate, but Leo asked someone to keep him in the loop."

"And they've just messaged me to say the girl didn't make it. It was Aimee," Leo admits.

My heart sinks, and my stomach twits as heat rushes over my skin, chased away by a cold sweat as my head swims. I thought this was over.

We were done.

Safe.

Only we're not.

The boys have been dragged in to prove their loyalty *one last time,* Penelope is missing, and now Aimee is dead. What the hell is going on here? Panic claws at the edge of my vision, ready to pull me under.

"Breathe, Ivy," Wyatt says, pressing his hands against my arms. "Just, breathe, baby girl. We've got you."

"How can you say that?" I clip out, my thoughts running a mile a minute. "They're picking us off one at a time. Nobody's safe."

"The Sect can't find Penelope—that's why Jacob is here. If they wanted to kill us all off, they had the three of us alone this afternoon to do just that," Wyatt explains slowly, waiting for each point to hit its mark before moving on to the next.

The intercom blares, and we're called down to dinner. I'm not sure food is something any of us can stomach right now, but together, we go, albeit sombrely. The guys are completely unsurprised to find the chief of police in the dining room when we get there, but my hesitation isn't missed.

I've met him a few times at events with my father, but what on earth is he doing here, and how is he wrapped up in all this?

"Chief," Nick says, coming to stand in front of me.

The chief notes the move with a smirk and the raise of an eyebrow before gesturing to the seats and waiting silently for us to join him.

"I'm sorry to inform you that Miss Warren has passed away under suspicious circumstances this afternoon," he says, confirming what we already know about Aimee. *He's part of The Sect.* "Your classes will be done from the house for the next few days, and all presentations, notes, and assignments will be sent to you virtually. You're not to leave this house, with the exception of Friday night's ceremony."

So, it wasn't them.

"Security will be posted at both entrances until your membership is finalised. This is the safest place for you all whilst we look into this further," he says, leaving the rest of us stunned into silence.

It's strange, but it almost sounds like he's concerned for our safety, but that can't be right… can it?

This has got to be another way for The Sect to control and manipulate us in these last few days. Yet there's something almost earnest in his tone. Something very close to him giving a shit.

"Everything is in place for the ceremony now, so there should be no need for anyone to leave. Findlay, Matthew, and your cleaning team will attend as normal, and your work can be completed in the office provided. If you need anything extra, you can ask security, but I make no promises," the chief says, standing before looking to me. "Hair and makeup will be here at seven on Friday."

"That's… uh, great. Yeah, thank you."

He nods, not waiting for any more conversation before making his way out. The door slams shut behind him, and the lock clicks into place with a finality we all feel, even from the dining room.

Dinner soon arrives, and with stilted conversation, we do our best to get through it, some of the excitement of Jacob's return tarnished by the bad news of Aimee's recent death and the turn of events it has caused.

What on earth is going on here?

THIRTEEN

Nick

"What happens now? Do we have to organise a funeral, or will her family do that?" Ivy asks, absentmindedly drawing patterns on my thigh.

"That all looked fairly public and official. I think it would be fair to say her family will be doing that," Wyatt says calmly.

"Unlike everyone else," Ivy replies.

I know that she means Charlotte's family, and not those of the people we… yeah, not the ones we saw this afternoon. She means the rest of the people we haven't seen. Even so, I can't help the twinge in my chest.

"How much longer do you think they'll be?" I ask, gesturing to the bathroom that Jacob and Leo disappeared into the second we got upstairs.

On cue, the door opens and the two of them join us on the sectional. Jacob looks more like himself for a second hot shower and some food, but something is still off, and I can't put my finger on it.

Perhaps it's just because I'm not the same after the stress of the last month spent without him, never mind everything else we've been through. Maybe it's something else entirely. Whatever it is, hopefully we'll be back to normal soon, because there aren't words for how grateful I was to come home and find my brother sitting in the kitchen with my girl.

"You feeling more like it?" Ivy asks Jacob.

"Definitely," he replies, gifting her a smile. "I'll never take comfy joggers for granted again."

It was surreal to come up here and find all his things exactly where he left them. It was almost like the last month never happened; except we all know it did.

"Well, now you guys have filled me in, I guess I'd better do the same," Jacob says, sucking a breath in. "As you can imagine, it's not been a bed of roses, but it definitely helped me to know that you guys were together and safe."

Leo squeezes his knee before adjusting their positions to lean back into the corner and pulling Jacob back against his chest, framing his legs with his own. It shouldn't work, my brother's broad frame being wrapped up by another man, but Leo isn't just any other man. As Jacob takes Leo's hand in his, it's also clear he needs the support to get whatever else he has to say to us out.

"I'm going to be honest, when I realised I was last and they escorted me out of that building, I wasn't sure I'd make it back to you." He swallows thickly, looking at Wyatt. "But I remembered what we'd talked about, and I knew you'd find a way," he admits, twisting the tracking bracelet Wyatt gave us around his wrist.

He can't say the words out loud, but he knew we'd do everything we could to get to him.

"It seemed to go on forever, those first few days… weeks, but I got your messages, your hopes and dreams, and they kept me going through everything."

Tears well in his eyes, and Ivy snuggles closer into my side, letting her strength pour into me. I need him to get through this. They're only words, and not nearly the worst of everything he's lived through recently.

"So, I chose to honour my oath to The Sect," Jacob continues, shaking whatever thoughts from his head. "There were some who didn't, and I can only assume they've ended up in that cemetery at the unmarked grave we saw. But I wasn't the only one."

We took the lives of those who didn't agree to honour their oaths only hours ago, but that was just three of them. What about everyone else?

"You weren't the only one, what? That was there?" Ivy asks, leaning forward. "Are you saying *everyone* was offered the opportunity to honour their oaths and work for The Sect? That... that Tamsin could still be alive?"

The yearning that clings to those words should be enough to make it true, but is it?

"I don't know exactly who accepted and who didn't. We weren't sitting around socialising in there, but there's a chance," Jacob admits.

"But, how? Why?"

"You took an oath at New Year's, just like we did before this all started, and there are only two ways to get out of it: death and excommunication," Wyatt says, repeating the same explanation we were given only hours ago.

"I chose to stay." Jacob says the words calmly, but the storm in his gaze tells me it was never that simple. "I don't think I was the only one who chose that."

"So, if you don't make it through the challenges, you still get the opportunity to work for The Sect, just not with all the glitz and glamour," Leo says, thinking aloud, the cogs turning behind his eyes. "They're the security that are everywhere, the drivers that keep turning up. Probably the staff at Pendleton Prep. Hell, maybe even the two guys who cook dinner each night."

"Because each Devil is hand-selected with a particular skillset in mind," Wyatt continues, putting all the pieces into place. "The non-bloodline recruits fill the gaps in their wider operation, because controlling the masses is done by the top one percent with support."

"But Tamsin never took an oath," Ivy argues, that hope she was holding onto faltering.

"No, but Taylor did. She linked her fate to his with that damn wristlet, and if he agreed to honour his oath, she could be still there. They both might be," I finish.

"And we know where this is, so we could go and get her… keep her safe," Ivy says, excitement pouring off her in waves.

"No easier than we could have done with Jacob," Leo says sadly, and all four of us watch as Ivy deflates before us, the reality of the situation tumbling around her.

"I'm here because The Sect need three Devils and three Angels to complete the initiation, and as an untied bloodline member, that gives me priority."

"So, will they bring someone else in now that Aimee is… has… now that Aimee isn't part of our final six?" Ivy asks, failing to finish the sentence the way she intended.

"Who else is there?" Wyatt asks. "Stephanie was

linked to Oliver." *And he's dead. They both are.* "Penelope is MIA." *That's why Jacob is here.* "Tamsin is linked to Taylor, Charlotte didn't make it through New Year's Eve, and then you're here. There isn't anyone else."

"They want us linking one Angel to one Devil, but if there's no one else for them to slide into our places, what are they going to do if we demand linking to all of you?" she asks. "What difference would it make?"

"I honestly don't know," Wyatt ponders. "But I guess we could find out."

"But this means that you're back-back. Like, for good back, right?" I confirm, looking at Jacob.

It's not that I don't care who ends up linked with who, it's just that, more than anything, I need to know I'm not going to wake up in the morning and find out this was all a dream or a joke, and that he's gone again. Sure, it's great that some of the other guys are out there somewhere. Even better for Ivy that Tamsin could be, too. It really doesn't bother me who Ivy links herself to because at the end of the day she's as much theirs as she is mine. Although my ego would probably argue that point. But what I really need to know is that we won't have to go through this bullshit again. That Jacob is here to stay.

"I'm not going anywhere," he confirms with a nod, a small smile playing on his lips. "So, if you'd all kindly remind me what the hell I was holding on for, that would be great."

Jacob grins, and Leo tightens his grip around him briefly as the two of them wait us out, watching for the moment the penny drops. The air in the room shifts when we realise

what he means: sex. Not just who he was holding on for…
but what.

"Are you honestly trying to tell me that Leo wasn't
showing you exactly how excited he is to have you back
home in that shower?" I ask, raising an eyebrow.

"And you're definitely not interested in anything I have
to offer," Ivy adds nervously.

"I think I remember saying something about loving you
all until death," Jacob counters. "And that means all of you,
one way or another."

"Then, what were you holding out for?" Leo asks, his
voice dropping an octave as he slides his fingers along the
edge of Jacob's sweatpants, the temperature in the room
increasing by the second.

"More than just your dick and his hard abs," Jacob
comments, looking at Wyatt.

The shock on Wyatt's face would be amusing if I could
work out what on earth Jacob was talking about.

"Yeah?" Leo's hand disappears in those same pants as
Ivy adjusts herself beside me, her gaze following my own.

"More than these?" Ivy asks, standing.

She takes the two steps to Wyatt, sliding her hands down
his chest before gripping the hem of his T-shirt and pulling it
up and over his head. She steps between his thighs, pulling
the band from his hair and running her fingers through it.

The rumble of appreciation that tumbles from Wyatt
sparks something, that simmering sizzle of anticipation
bursting to life.

Jacob swallows hard before he replies with a throaty,
"Yes."

With a nod, Ivy ties Wyatt's hair back up, turning to me with a wicked glint in her eye. She rips my shirt off, too, discarding it with Wyatt's before adding her own to the foray, her perfect skin glistening in the dim light of the room.

"You're all important to me, and even though I have no desire to be the man who brings you all to ecstasy," Jacob says, biting his lip as his eyes close and his hips buck into Leo's hand before he continues, heat blaring through his stare as he locks his gaze on Ivy. "I still want to be part of it when you fall apart. I want to see my grumpy brother brought to his knees by this beautiful spitfire of a woman and the two other men that care for her as much as I do. I want it all."

It could be beautiful, poetic almost, but all I take from his words are the raw hunger for the people he thought he'd lost. The love and affection he thought he'd never be able to feel again. But we're here, together. Finalists at last. All of us.

"Take his shirt off, sugar," I whisper to Ivy.

He wants us to worship her, for him to be a part of something bigger than just his own pleasure. Well, we can give him that.

Leo's hand snakes out of Jacob's pants as Ivy steps towards them, a shiver of anticipation rippling over Jacob when she whispers something to him before sliding the shirt off his beautiful body, with Leo's coming off behind him and landing somewhere on the floor between us all.

"You should see the two of them fuck her," I comment, picturing her coming undone with her lips wrapped around my cock, and both Leo and Wyatt buried deep inside of her. "It was breathtaking."

Jacob quirks an eyebrow as he looks up at Ivy as a blush graces her cheeks that matches the flush covering Jacob's when Leo pluck's his nipple.

"Who knew you could let go of the reins?" Jacob asks with a smirk.

Ivy snorts out a laugh before peeking over her shoulder at me and pressing her lips together in a way that has me wanting to sink my teeth into the soft flesh and watch her wriggle and writhe as I do it. After unfastening my jeans, I slide them and my boxers off, kicking them away and palming my dick. I let the two of them enjoy her last time. It's my turn now.

Taking the challenge in my gaze personally, Ivy turns, sashaying her way towards me on slow, precise, delicate steps. Her hips sway tantalisingly as her luscious breasts bob and bounce with each perfectly placed movement, making my lips dry, and my throat parched.

She stops just a step away, placing her hands on her hips and cocking an eyebrow. "I thought I was the one bringing you to your knees, not the other way around." She throws the words down, popping the catch on her soft, black trousers and waiting.

The rest of the room becomes nothing but background noise as I lean forward, my dick standing at full attention as I force myself to slow, not wanting the rest of them to see exactly how desperate I am for her. Sliding my hands up the outside of her thighs, I sink to my knees, grabbing a handful of her arse and squeezing the firm globe as I press my face into her pussy and breathe in deeply, the hot air rushing back out against her most intimate parts.

Slowly sliding the zipper down, and pushing the soft fabric off her hips, I leave it to pool at her feet, my panted breaths skimming against her thighs as she waits patiently for whatever I decide to do next.

What I want to do is bend her over the arm of the sofa and ram my dick so hard and fast into her that she feels me for the next three days, but Jacob wants to see her come undone, and she wants me to worship her, so a feast on my knees it is.

I pull one leg over my shoulder, doing my best to ignore the pulsing of my dick as I slide my tongue along her lace-covered pussy. Her salty taste bursts on my tongue as I go lower, letting the lace rub up and down against her clit while I feast, pushing it inside her as I spear her with my tongue, my fingers tracing light patterns against her clit.

Her hands thread in my hair, desperately attempting to keep herself upright when I shove the soaked scrap of lace to the side and continue in earnest. I'm more than ready for what I hope to be her first orgasm of many to be at my hands, and I don't have to wait long before she shudders and shakes, her walls clamping down on my fingers as I suck her clit.

"Fuck," she pants. "Sit back. I need you inside me."

Not one to deny such an offer, I shuffle backwards, barely getting my arse on the sofa before she's climbing into my lap and impaling herself on me. Her wet heat envelopes me, and the moan we share echoes around the all too quiet room.

"Someone get the lube," I manage to grit out before sucking a perfect, pink nipple into my mouth.

"Oh, God," Ivy moans, her head dropping back as she grinds in my lap clearly enjoying the thought of what's to come.

"Wyatt fucked you there last time. Do you want him again, sugar? Or can you take Leo?" I ask.

There's no way there'll ever be a dick measuring contest here, but there was something different about the way her body arched over Leo as he slid inch after inch inside her. The angle, the size, the shape. I honestly have no desire to overthink it, but I do want her to feel good, and as much as there's a fine line between pain and pleasure, I'm not sure that's one she wants to explore right now.

A bottle lands at my side, and before I've had chance to move, Ivy's being pulled over me as Wyatt's lips crash into hers. Her nails dig into my chest as her pussy squeezes the life out of me. Her rocking and rolling stutters as she comes again, Wyatt's surprisingly demanding kiss tipping her over the edge.

On panted breaths, she pulls back, her body softening as the frantic edge finally leaves her bones, but we're not done yet.

"Leo," Wyatt declares. "These lips are mine."

He climbs over the sofa, sitting on the back of it with his trousers undone but still on as he returns to kissing the ever-loving fuck out of Ivy. I gently roll my hips, doing everything I can think of to not fuck her into next week and come all over her beautiful skin, claiming her as my own.

Over her shoulder, Leo and Jacob share a moment,

no words needing to be said before Jacob stands, turning to offer his hands out to Leo, and that's when I see them. Thick, red marks criss-crossed over his back.

I don't even realise I'm frozen still and absolutely fuming until the rage pumping through my veins tumbles out of my mouth on a growl. "Who the hell did that to you?"

Leo offers a sympathetic look as Wyatt and Ivy pull apart, our lust-filled bubble popping as they, too, take in the destruction that used to be my brother's perfect skin.

"Not now," Jacob pleads. "We're not doing this now."

Lava runs through my body, and I remove my hands from Ivy's before I mark her, before I hurt her, but nobody moves. We barely breathe.

"I'm here. Can we please just remember who and what we are to each other," Jacob asks, his vulnerability laid out for all to see.

Leo places a kiss to the side of one of the marks, bringing his lips to Jacob's as he manoeuvres him, taking the source of my anger from my current line of sight. This is what they were communicating about. Leo already knew, and now he needs us to show Jacob that he's just as amazing as he was before The Sect got their hands on him.

Wyatt flicks the lid open on the lube and offers it out to Leo, an apology on the tip of his tongue. If he'd not claimed Ivy's lips as his own, I may have been too distracted to notice what they've done to Jacob.

"Maybe Nick here needs reminding that we are all alive and here together right now," Wyatt says, his voice carrying over to Jacob and Leo as they close the distance between us.

Ivy drops her arms over my shoulders, her lips pressing

against mine as her tongue reignites the spark between us and, sadly, I realise they're right. Jacob doesn't want to talk about it, to explain it. He wants to see us worship our Angel. For all five of us to come together like only we can now our missing link is back.

I can't do anything about what's happened whilst he's been away from us, and certainly not right now. Especially when he wants to focus on the moment. So, I let myself tumble back into it, enjoying the press of Ivy's supple body against mine, the feel of Leo stretching her tight hole as she grinds down against me, a mewl tumbling from her.

"Are you just observing, or were you planning on taking part here?" I ask Jacob as he sits across from us, concern followed by heat flickering across his face, along with a whole bunch of emotions I can't catch before they're gone.

Slowly but surely, Leo works Ivy over, the low moan that falls from her as he finally pushes in seeming to spur both Jacob and Wyatt on. The three of us do our best to find a rhythm, with Leo pulling back as I press forward, and Ivy's nails digging into my chest as she catches Wyatt's lips in a searing kiss.

Leo twitches and groans as Jacob enters him, twisting him almost inhumanely to kiss him sloppily, and when Wyatt finally releases his cock from the confines of his pants, Ivy wraps her fist around it with an ease I wasn't expecting.

"You good?" I ask her, pinching a nipple whilst doing my best to not blow my load.

"Yes," Ivy pants, her lips coming to mine as Jacob's hard thrusts push Leo deeper into her arse, and she climbs ever nearer to the peak we're all teetering on.

"Harder," Wyatt moans, bucking his hips. "Grip me tighter."

Jacob's hand snakes around, and he wraps his fingers over Ivy's to help her pump Wyatt's cock in time with his thrusts.

"Oh, fuck." The words tumble out on an exhale as Wyatt looks down, following the line of Jacob's thick, tanned fingers up his arm, until the two of them hold gazes, and Wyatt comes hard—hot jets spurting out that Ivy quickly moves to lap up.

The desperate lathe of her tongue and the change of angle has me coming undone, coming hard deep inside her as she clamps down around me and sets off a chain reaction, making Leo and then Jacob fall over the cliff with us.

We're a hot, sweaty tangle of limbs as, one by one, we unlink, and Ivy stands on shaky legs before falling back into my lap, sated.

"Nice to have you back," Ivy says to Jacob between breaths, winking his way.

Leo disappears to grab a cloth, but before he returns, Wyatt drags Ivy from my lap, laying her out on the sofa and throwing her legs over his shoulders, fanning his breath over her sensitive skin.

I'm not the only one held rapt as Jacob drops to the edge of the sofa, watching Wyatt slide his fingers through the come leaking from our girl. He gathers it together as Ivy's legs tremble, pushing it deeper into her pulsating pussy.

The moan that falls from her has us all half-hard again. Wyatt presses soft kisses against her clit as I do my best to press my hard-on back down. Leo returns, a warm cloth in hand, but when he sees how Ivy is currently tangled up, he heads straight for Jacob, sinking to his knees and cleaning his cock before he, too, wraps his lips around him. Jacob's moans of pleasure tangle in the air with Ivy's.

It's more than just sex, and more than the physical act of the five of us coming together again, re-learning each other's bodies, and figuring out how we all fit. It's the joining of our most intimate parts, our hopes, our fears.

We'll no longer have to worry about losing a part of ourselves. We'll never have to consider life without one of us, because this is it. The five of us together, against the world, until death. It's the joining of souls, the creating of life.

"Take mine, too," Wyatt says roughly as he enters Ivy, his measured strokes working her up again.

"Fuck," I manage to grind out, my cock dying for another taste of her sweet pussy, but making do with the way I grip it myself, the sound, sights, and smell of sex in the air intoxicating.

Jacob and I have had sex with groups before, once or twice, but never anything as involved as this, and only ever as a one-off. But every time the five of us tumble together, they steal another part of me.

Sooner or later, I'm not going to be able to tell where they start and I end, and I can't say it frightens me in the slightest. In fact, now Jacob's back, I'm more than happy to hand every part of myself to them for safekeeping.

"Yes, all of you," Ivy cries, her body bowing beneath Wyatt's. "I need all of you."

"You guys ready to indulge our girl?" Wyatt asks over

his shoulder, slowing his pace as Ivy growls in frustration, clawing at the cushion beneath her.

Like a siren's call, I join the two of them, continuing to work my dick in time to Wyatt's lazy thrusts, the three of us growing more impatient by the second. Ivy whimpers as I wrap my lips around a pert pink nipple, her fingers sinking into my hair as she teeters back on the edge of oblivion.

"Let me taste you," she purrs, reaching for my cock.

Releasing her, I move, sliding my thick length into the heat of her mouth, her moan reverberating all the way down to my toes. This isn't going to take long.

"Leo," I manage to croak out. "Make him feel good and bring everything he deigns to feed you over here."

She's already full of mine and Leo's come, and Wyatt's hanging on by a thread. The only one left out here is the man who holds us all together. And whilst he has zero desire to feel the exhalation of her amazing pussy clamping down around him, there's more than one way to get her what she wants: all of us.

Brushing my fingers over her clit has Ivy's eyes rolling back in her head, and as Wyatt picks up his pace, I'm almost ready to combust.

She moans again, her nails digging into my thigh as her legs clamp down against Wyatt, holding him captive as another orgasm wracks through her body and a flush creeps over her collarbone. Seconds later, I follow her over the hill, with Wyatt not far behind me, landing back on his heels. Then my gaze turns to Leo and Jacob.

The lust in Jacob's gaze as it flicks from Leo to the three of us and back is more than I expected, and when his thrusts stutter and stop, I call out to remind Leo that we need him.

"Open your legs, sugar," I purr, sitting back on the end of the sectional and pulling Ivy's back against my chest.

Her legs flop over each of mine, my dick pressed between the two of us as Leo's heated gaze travels over us both. He drops to his knees, pulling Ivy's pussy down to his face before squirting Jacob's come inside her, lapping up what comes back out before pushing that in, too.

If she doesn't end up with a tiny version of one of us after this then I have no idea what it would take, but there's no denying she's ours as much as we're hers, now and always.

"That's it, angel. Take us all," Leo says, looking up at her with wonder in his eyes.

"Fuck, that was…" Her sentence trails off as a satisfied shiver ripples over her body.

"Awesome?" Wyatt offers.

"Hot?" Jacob continues.

"Fucking amazing," Ivy finishes, closing her thighs and curling into my body.

Jacob smiles, scooping her out of my arms and walking her to the bed, whispering quietly to her as he wraps the covers around her. But the marks on his back make anger bubble beneath the surface of my skin, once again.

Leo catches the change in me, promising a trip to the gym in the morning. "Just give them tonight, yeah?"

Nodding, I agree. How could I take this moment from Jacob, from Ivy, from all of us?

I pass him, slapping a hand on his shoulder before joining Wyatt as he climbs into bed, tangling his legs with

Ivy's, and sliding an arm under her head. Getting in behind her, I wrap myself around her back, the big spoon to her little one, waiting for Leo to find his place.

Everything else will wait, because right now, we're together, and we have peace.

FOURTEEN

Ivy

The den has been transformed into nothing short of a beauty salon as I loiter awkwardly in the doorway, the three black-clad women going about their set-up, oblivious to the nerves that eat away at me as I stand just a few feet away from them.

We've never had this kind of effort made.

The first time we were called to The Sect, all the girls got together and brought our own hair stylists, nail techs, and makeup artists. We made it a fun afternoon of preparation whilst we got to know each other a little better.

Sadly, that didn't last, and by the time the New Year's party rolled around, it was just four of us getting ready together, the excitement well and truly worn off.

Now, here we are, at the end. Only Jacob and I left for the Angels, and they send a team of professionals to us for the finale. I suppose it's because they can't trust anyone at the moment, because we aren't allowed to leave the house, and the only people coming in are vetted and approved by The Sect.

I shouldn't complain, it's a nice gesture, but it certainly

raises questions about the expectations of this evening. If they've gone to this amount of trouble to get us ready, what else is in store?

"Come on, let's get this over with," Jacob grumbles from behind me, placing his hands on my waist as he uses me like a human shield, pushing us into the room.

We're quietly guided to the two mirrored stations set up, and my hair is released from its messy bun as the unknown woman runs her fingers through it, teasing a tangle or two as she tilts her head from side to side.

The black face covering hides any thoughts she has, the light veil over her eyes disguising any interest before she gestures to the sink for me to move and lean back. Quickly and quietly, she washes my hair, massaging my scalp, and almost making me forget where we are and the worry of what's to come.

"This seems like a lot," I comment, getting back in the seat beside Jacob as his stylist snips away carefully at the ends of his hair.

"We're finalists now." He shrugs, catching my gaze through the mirror. "They've got to keep us locked up tight, safe, ready for showing off to the world."

The stylist begins blow-drying my hair, and any further conversation we might have had falls to the wayside, but something about his choice of words sticks with me. What if keeping us safe here means that The Sect haven't sent their usual outsourced people?

When we held the spa day with the Little Sisters at the pool house, none of the technicians there were hidden or covered because they weren't staff from The Sect. They were 'normal' people. So, if The Sect is currently worried about safety, what if they're using their internal *staff*?

Jacob said there were others in the place they kept him: drivers, security, muscle… but there's got to be women there, too, hasn't there? The Angels that were paired up… like Tamsin. What if one of these women is Tamsin?

Suddenly, I'm overanalysing every look, every movement. I'd know if my best friend was standing right here, wouldn't I?

Jacob is different now, but still so much the same. There's a shadow hanging over him after everything he's been through, the worst of which I'm sure he hasn't yet shared. He may not ever. But he's still very much himself in so many ways. The mannerisms haven't changed.

As the woman trims and styles Jacob's hair, I watch, observe, quietly trying to work out if she could be someone I know. Someone I care about and lost.

"It looks like Nick and Leo have got over themselves," Jacob comments as the stylist sweeps foundation over his face.

"Yeah, that's been an evolution," I agree, watching the woman behind me through the mirror as she places what has to be the final pin in my hair. "Don't get me wrong, they've been at each other's throats some of the time, too, but they're definitely working together much better."

My stylist swaps places with the third one—the lady who's been silent and still in the corner this entire time. She takes a quick look over the flowers in my hair before reaching for a moisturiser and starting on my makeup.

"To be honest, they spent the first week or two kicking

seven shades out of each other in the ring. Then Wyatt intervened, and the three of them have become a bit of a unit," I admit.

It's been a rocky month, and there have been a few moments when I'd wondered just how much damage they could do to each other and still continue to pick each other up at the end of the day. Or how much pain and endurance they could inflict on themselves before they finally snapped. To say I was grateful when Wyatt stepped in would be an understatement.

"Once the weather gets better, I'm looking forward to getting back out for a run or two. The treadmill isn't the same, and being trapped in this house is driving me crazy."

"It's only been three days," Jacob reminds me with a quirk of his eyebrow.

His stylist steps back, gesturing to the robes that hang beside a decorative screen. They've done nothing more than style his hair and cover the obvious sleep deprivation that still marks his perfect face, but he looks more like himself for it—refreshed, even.

"I'm almost done," the stylist tells me as she does her best to avoid looking me in the eye while she lines my lips, but it's the hissed intake of breath she takes when Jacob takes off his shirt, the once angry marks making an appearance until he slides the simple white cotton shirt over them, that makes me look at her closer.

I know The Sect is panicked, closing the ranks and the doors, but would they really send someone we know so closely to us now… so soon?

She didn't think twice about the shade of foundation or

the type of serum to use, reaching for the right one's like we've done this together a million times before. And the knowing pain as she looked at Jacob… has that been done to her, too? To someone she cares about?

The black robes hide everything. No hint of a shape, figure, or her height can be garnered as I look at each of them again earnestly. They could have flats on, or heels, and the loose material covers everything, the grey veil obscuring even their eyes. But as I look closely, I know it's not her. Not my Tamsin.

The shape of the eyes is wrong, the colour nowhere near, and despite the hope that blossomed momentarily that she could still be alive and be here, I know she isn't. Maybe she is somewhere, but not with me right now.

Whatever these women have seen and have been through, it's enough to have her scuttle back, gesturing for me to change without a single word being spoken.

They know we're still being watched and listened to. Even if they wanted to reassure us or warn us of what's to come, they couldn't do so without repercussion. I'm quietly confident that's not something any of us want.

If the women who survive this ordeal are those linked to a Devil at some point, then it's not only their lives they have to worry about.

Jacob clips the cloak into place, one of the stylists adjusting it over his shoulders before placing my robes on the other side of the screen for me. She follows, folding my clothes as I peel them off, placing the simple shirt and trousers on, then wrapping the cloak around me.

Unexpectedly, she reaches inside the heavy material,

adjusting one of the folds before discreetly pushing a scrap of paper into my fingers. Avoiding my gaze, she steps back, walking away from me as the paper burns in my hand.

My heart pounds, and my mouth is suddenly dry as I unfold it as quietly as I can manage, the red outline of a single heart drawn on a scrap of toilet paper. It could be blood or it could be lipstick. It's clearly whatever she had access to in the moment, but this is what Tamsin and I used to pass each other in class.

She's alive… somewhere, and she knew these women were coming here tonight.

Shoving the paper in my pocket, I adjust the front fastening, then step out, my mask in hand, as I shove the elation deep, deep down. I'll find her and get her safe, too, but for now, I need to get through one last night with The Sect.

FIFTEEN

Nick

Jacob's presence at my side does very little to alleviate the tension coiled through my every muscle as I fix the black cloak into place, the pin catching yet again. With nothing more than a roll of his eyes, he flicks my fingers out of the way and closes the catch with practiced ease.

"Have you spoken to Sophie?" I ask quietly.

"Of course. She told me to let you know that their winnings arrived safely in Italy. She was obviously excited to hear from her favourite baby brother, but I'm reasonably sure she knew I wouldn't be able to go into details."

"Considering the secrets they've been keeping, I'm not surprised. Actually, how far did you get in the New Year's Revelations thing? Do you know the things I know?" I ask.

"About blood being thicker than water, and our fun family ties? Oh, yeah. I know all about those," he replies, turning away.

"And the video?" I ask. The one our father made before he passed away, telling us he was proud of who we've become and to keep going. I don't want to rub it in if he didn't see it, but it would be good to know that he had something to hold on to.

"I saw the video," he says with a nod, just as Ivy comes in.

Her makeup is subtle but enhancing in all the right paces, her hair half-braided and wrapped in a bunch of flowers, making her look like the embodiment of springtime.

"No flowers for you?" I ask, looking at Jacob, even as I close the distance between Ivy and me.

"Not enough hair to pin it into," she replies with a small smile, drawing my attention back to the woman who holds my heart captive.

It's taken a few days for it to feel real. Jacob's back, and we're all together. The people who were trying to tear us apart, and worse, are gone, and despite my momentary hesitance, in the end, finishing Oliver's life isn't haunting me.

I don't wake up in a cold sweat picturing Oliver's face, or Stephanie's, or George's. No, I take solace in the knowledge that none of them would have thought twice if the shoe had been on the other foot. Plus, they were shitty people, and even worse teammates. We're better off without them. The whole world is.

That's not to say that Wyatt hasn't woken up in the middle of the night looking lost and confused, but a few calming words from Leo or me, and a stroke of Ivy's perfect skin between us, and he soon settles again. It's clearly taking him longer to come to terms with it, but we did the only thing we could.

I think, if anything, the forced proximity of the last few days has been more of an issue. Jacob's here… but he's not the same. I guess we knew things would be different, but it's hard, and reaching him is proving tricker than anticipated. I've spent so much time over the last month worrying about getting him back, but I never spent any of that time thinking about which parts of him would return.

"I'll grow it out for the next one." Jacob winks, some of his usual charm showing through as he smooths his favourite moisturiser over his hands.

"There's not going to be a next one," I clip out. "This is it. Done."

Ivy rubs soothing circles on my chest, pulling me back from the edge of panic when thoughts of him being taken away again cause my heartbeat to race, and my fists to clench.

We won't be pulled apart again. Divided. Separated.

If they thought driving a wedge between us would work, they've vastly underestimated the bond between the Barrett twins. He won't be leaving my line of sight any time soon. Not if I have anything to say about it.

"You do look fresh and glowing, though," Ivy says to Jacob, pressing her lips to my cheek before sliding past me.

As I look closer at Jacob, I realise she's right. I thought it was just the doing of a couple of nights of good sleep and decent food, but whatever pampering they've been having has made a big difference. Turns out it's going to take more than sleep and food for my brother to look himself again. It's going to take a whole bunch of makeup I didn't even realise he was wearing.

"Thank you," Jacob replies with a wink.

The door closes behind him when he leaves. Ivy

is picking out the last of the jewellery she wants for this evening. I can't explain or control it, but I have the irrational desire to rip every piece of clothing off her body—clothing someone else chose for her—but I push it to one side because there's no way in hell she's going to be allowed to meet The Sect without their requested attire.

No doubt if I got rid of this one, they'd have a spare set magically appear from nowhere. Well, I suppose there are both Aimee and Penelope's hanging up downstairs. Neither of them are going to be able to wear them now.

"What ya thinking?" Ivy asks with a cheeky grin, popping up right in front of me and drawing my attention back to the here and now and the good things we've got right in front of us.

"Oh, just about how criminal it is to cover up those beautiful curves," I bluff, even if it is the truth.

She pops the hood of her cloak up, swinging the white Angel mask from her fingers as she tugs my black one up to match.

"Are you ready for this?" she asks, the one question I've been asking myself since we walked out of the old church a few days ago.

This is it. Am I ready?

"Got to be, sugar," I reply.

Her hands hang over my shoulders, her heels almost bringing her to my height as she reads every truth I can't speak out loud in my eyes. I lay it all out for only her to see: the fear, the hope, the anger, the helplessness. It's all sitting right on the surface for just a moment.

A blink and she'd have missed it, but she didn't.

Instead, she wraps her arms around me, pulling me ever closer, bringing her lips to mine. Conscious of the hour she spent getting ready and the countdown we're under, I don't attempt to deepen it, no matter how much I want to.

Sure, turning up to the ceremony with lipstick smeared over her face and mascara tracks down her cheeks would definitely be one way to go, but there will be time for that later. Despite the urge, we need to keep The Sect on side. They hold our lives in their hands… for now.

Pulling back, I press our foreheads together, leaving my eyes closed for just another moment, an extra second of peace before we walk straight into Hell.

"Let's get this over with," I grumble, aware of the itch under my skin now that Jacob has moved into the other room.

"We've got this," she says decidedly. "Together, to love, to care for, to protect, until death."

"Until death," I agree.

Although I'm coming to realise there are things in life far worse than death.

The three of us make our way downstairs, meeting Wyatt and Leo in the entrance with their black masks already in place. The gold slash across mine is reflected in Jacob's white one, but the red in Leo's and the silver of Wyatt's is nowhere to be seen in Ivy's plain white mask. The one that makes her deep red lipstick stand out even more now the top half of her face is covered.

"You guys look eerie as fuck," Ivy comments once I slide my mask on. "God, I can't wait for this to be over." Her final words are whispered, her nerves showing through just for us.

And it is almost over, at last.

The door opens before The Sect's security guide us to two waiting cars, with Ivy and Jacob going in one, Wyatt, Leo and I being ushered into the other. Luckily, the cars stay together as we make our way to the old church, nerves eating their way through my stomach as the seconds tick by.

The car park is surprisingly full, and as we're directed to a side door rather than the main entrance, those nerves solidify into a lump at the back of my throat, helplessness threatening to swallow me whole when the door finally locks behind us.

This is it. We're trapped inside the building. The only way out is back through two security guards and a locked door. The only way forward is through an entire secret society. If they decide we haven't made the cut and want to end us, there is next to nothing we could do about it.

We've always been the main attraction; the centre of attention. Even when we were in challenges it was about us, both individually and as a group, but losing Jacob has opened my eyes to so many of the little things I've missed before.

We have never been in control of this process. We've been passed around, pushed along from one thing to the next, the centre of attention only by their design, and now we're being delivered through a dank corridor and told to wait for our moment.

I haven't been able to do anything about losing our friends through this, but I tried everything I could think of to keep us together, to keep us whole, even when that's fallen short. Whatever happens tonight, if it goes wrong, it will be me. Not Leo. Not Jacob. Not Wyatt or Ivy.

If someone has to go, if something has to give, it will be me, because I couldn't live with myself, or with them, if it wasn't. If I failed to protect someone else. Again.

After being shoved into an antechamber, we are lined up and told to wait as a voice speaks on the other side of the wall, the words indiscernible, unlike the light that filters through when the door opens and security gesture us through.

"The finalists from Pendleton Prep!" is announced as we wander onto the raised platform, five seats waiting for us as this evening's master of ceremonies gestures for us to sit.

The room is packed, almost as busy as that first night when we were introduced, although there are a lot less of 'us' now than there used to be. There are a mix of people wearing masks and some forgoing them, but it's clear there are no wives or girlfriends here tonight. This isn't some fancy show event. This is a transfer of power.

"Oaths have been sealed, and with the change of plans this week, blood sacrifices have already been made. So, the only thing remaining is to bond our new recruits into The Sect," the announcer continues, stepping closer to Leo.

My fingers itch as I look out over the masses of people before us, someone else moving around behind us just out of my line of vision until he steps beside the master of ceremonies with a silver tray in his hand.

"Red, the line of Windsor. Bold and vengeful. We welcome you, Leo Windsor, into our ranks," he says, plucking a vial from the tray before slowly pouring red oil down the front of Leo's mask. "In time, you will take over the work your father is currently undertaking, stepping up to be the underground contact for The Sect, procuring anything and everything we need. Until such a time is determined, you will continue with your studies and building contacts to further our great plans."

Sparing him a glance, I see the oil settling into the crevices and marks of his mask, making him look more gruesome than ever. The warrior of our little unit.

"Silver, the line of Chambers. Calculating and shrewd. We welcome you, Wyatt Chambers, into our ranks," the compare continues, a small vial cascading flecks of silver down Wyatt's mask. "Your great knowledge of numbers and patterns will come in very useful as the head of one or more of our business endeavours. In addition to the courses you are currently undertaking, formal management training will be introduced ready for you to take the helm as C.E.O."

Then he comes to stand behind me, his presence heady.

"Gold, the line of Barrett. Opulent and possessive. We welcome you, Nicholas Barrett, into our ranks." The oil is lightly scented, the gold flakes sticking to my cheeks and neck as it flows down and settles into my collar. "You have an interesting combination of attributes, but your work in law has been most thought provoking. Once the correct courses have been completed, a role as a judge will be your future."

He turns away from the three of us like he hasn't just handed us both our dreams and nightmares on a plate, focusing on Jacob and Ivy now.

"Ivy Rose Collins, which Devil are you linked with?"

he asks.

Collins… Like Deputy Mayor Collins? No, it can't be…

"My heart lies with Leo Windsor, Wyatt Chambers, and Nicholas Barrett," Ivy replies, her chin held high.

This is what she was talking about the other day.

If there is no one else to step in and take their spaces, take *our* spaces, then why can't she be linked to all three of us? What are they going to do, choose for her?

"Those are three very different life choices, Miss Collins," the compare comments with a dark chuckle. "It will not be possible for you to follow all three where they are going."

His pompous attitude and the way he sneers at her gets my back up, and as I turn to glower in his direction, Ivy takes us all by surprise.

"Respectfully, it is down to us to work out the logistics of that," she replies curtly.

Whispers break out in the ranks before us, but one person catches my eye as he leans casually against a column, an impressed smile on his face.

"Ivy Rose Collins, your life will be guided by the lines of Windsor, Chambers, and Barrett," the compare declares after a moment's deliberation, all three oils being poured liberally over her formerly pristine white mask before he moves over to Jacob, and my heart pounds.

He wasn't supposed to be here. They've already made that clear. So, what happens now?

If I thought I was nervous when he hovered behind Ivy, I was wrong. It's so much worse when he loiters near the other part of me—the part that I've only just got back. The threat so very real.

"Jacob Barrett, as a bloodline member, you are already tied to your household, but which Devil are you linked with?"

He doesn't hesitate. Doesn't even breathe before calmly replying, "My heart lies with Leo Windsor, Wyatt Chambers, and Nicholas Barrett."

I think it's safe to say whoever drew the short straw overseeing tonight is less than impressed with us when he pours the red and silver oils over Jacob's mask declaring, "Jacob Barrett, your life will be guided by the lines of Windsor, Chambers, and Barrett."

He steps back, a round of applause breaking out from the gathered crowd as they make their way up to greet us, with Leo and Wyatt's fathers being the first.

They share quiet words with their sons before wishing me congratulations and shaking my hand. Leo's father walks away quietly, but some other people go on to greet Jacob and Ivy, too. The two of them loiter at the side, the flowers in Ivy's hair and the smile on my brother's face all I really need to get me through this.

A deep-voiced masked man shakes my hand, wishing me congratulations.

"I've been rooting for you," he says, the voice familiar. Familiar because this is the guy who's been to the house once or twice—the one who keeps his mask on to protect us.

"Thank you," I reply.

"These are passed from father to son, and yours was sent to me for safekeeping when your father received his diagnosis," he says, pressing something small into my fingers.

Turning the black cygnet ring over in my hand, I recognise the markings instantly, and surprise colours my features. It's a ring my father used to wear—something I never understood the significance of until now.

"If I'm being honest, I was expecting something more permanent. Tattoos… branding, perhaps." I cringe, picturing all the weird and wonderfully torturous ways I thought they would claim us as part of this secret society.

"It wouldn't be very secret if we painted it on your body, would it?" he replies with a smile.

"Good point," I concede, sliding the ring onto my right middle finger.

"I can arrange for it to be re-sized if needed."

"No, it's fine. This is good," I say, turning it around on my finger and testing the resistance against my knuckle. This would probably not be my first choice, but it works. "What would have happened if both Jacob and I made it through as Devils?" I question, my gaze flicking to where my brother whispers to Ivy, the two of them smiling at whatever joke he had to share.

"Another would have been made for your line, but only one would go on for future considerations," he says, pressing his palms together before rubbing his hands in a nervous gesture I can't seem to place, yet it feels so familiar. "I'd better go and congratulate your fellow associates, but I look forward to seeing what you go on to do."

He slaps a hand down on my shoulder with a grin before stepping away and closing the few steps to Leo when I notice the matching ring on his hand. I guess it makes sense that all three of us get one, and now that it's all official, their fathers can pass their rings down.

A pang of disappointment twists in my gut, but only for a moment. Our father wasn't himself in those last few weeks—certainly not the man Jacob and I got a glimpse of in the videos we were shown. He knew we were coming here, knew we'd go far, and he'd prepared for everything accordingly, even going so far as to hand over his ring. He'd be proud of us, of that I'm one hundred percent sure.

Our relationship status on the other hand… well, that could have been a harder sell. Although Sophie didn't seem to question it too much. There was a raised eyebrow here or there, and a confused smirk from her fiancé, but then, I can't imagine he's much of an exhibitionist. Not that I want to linger on that thought too long.

The 'welcomes' and 'nice works' seem to go on forever, but eventually, the last person has said their piece and left us to it when the chief of police comes over to gather us all together.

"Someone will take you all back tonight, but I'm disbanding the rest of the security at the house. Now that you're sworn members of The Sect, you won't have any problems," he says with a definitive nod.

"So, this is it. We're done?" Leo confirms, and whilst the rest of the world wouldn't notice it, I see the edge of concern that crosses his face, the way his gaze keeps flicking to Jacob and Ivy unintentionally. There have been so many moments when we thought it was over only to find ourselves thrust in the middle of something else. I totally understand wanting to get absolute confirmation.

"You're officially members now. Your initiation is complete," the chief confirms with a nod.

The collective sigh of relief is embarrassing. They've already declared it, showed us off, and then everyone has spent the last who knows how long congratulating us. You'd think that would have been enough for it to sink it, but apparently not.

"Enjoy your evening, gentlemen… and lady. You've got classes to pass," he adds with a wink, handing us off to one of the drivers before disappearing into the throng of people loitering around.

Without any further pomp or ceremony, we load up and head home, keen to get these oil-stained robes off.

SIXTEEN

Ivy

My core pulses with the most delicious ache as I stretch my back, unintentionally arching against Nick's morning wood, but he doesn't stir too much. He just pulls me back into his heat. I should take the reprieve, enjoy the calm that comes before the storm, but I'm awake, and no amount of pretending is making me any sleepier.

"Morning, angel," Leo whispers, catching my gaze over Wyatt's shoulder.

He finishes whatever he's doing on his phone before sliding it onto the bedside table, his arm resting lightly on Jacob's shoulder, and a shuddered breath escapes his parted lips.

"Did you manage any sleep?" I ask, taking in his dishevelled state.

"Between the two of them tossing and turning? Not really."

A sigh escapes him, something contented yet defeated at the same time.

"It's just going to take time," I whisper, reaching over

to take his other hand and resting them on Wyatt's hip as he catches up on the sleep he's been so deprived of this week. "We're all just waiting for the other shoe to drop, but it'll get better."

I don't know if it helped to have it confirmed that they've been watching and listening to us this whole time, and I'm not convinced anyone really believes that dropping some oil over us really makes that much of a difference. Is that honestly enough for them to trust us? I guess it must be.

It feels like I took that oath a lifetime ago, the guys even further back, and even after that, they've watched us, waiting for someone to trip, for them to catch us in a lie or a mistake. It's hard to believe that the kind of trust you'd need to build to get out of such control can be provided by what we've been through this week. That the threat following one of our members going missing, and one killed, without any sort of explanation has suddenly disappeared because we're now official members of The Sect. Does it really make that much of a difference? Are we different now, too? How would anyone know?

"You're safe now; we all are," Leo says, squeezing my hand, fondness radiating from him as he looks across the pile of bodies curled together in our bed. "So, what have you got planned for the day?"

"Lunch with Ruby for me," I reply. "You?"

"Feed Jacob, kick the shit out of Nick, and help Wyatt work out what needs coordinating for his management training," he says, ticking the items off like he's been going over the list in his head for the last half an hour.

"Is that what you were looking up on your phone?"

"Amongst other things," he replies, one side of his mouth kicking up into a knowing smile that makes my thighs clench and my heart pound.

"Oh, yeah?"

"If we're not being watched any more, there are a few *accessories* I'd like to have on hand."

"Do you honestly believe the bullshit they spouted about this all being over?" I ask, taken aback.

Of all the people I thought might have bought into that, Leo isn't one. I'd like to think this means we're free and clear, but I'm not naive enough to believe it just like that.

"Yeah, I think so. He had no reason to lie to us."

"I'll believe it when I see it," I grumble.

But before we have time to delve any further into it, Wyatt wakes up between us, rubbing the sleep from his eyes, and pulling me into his chest before claiming my lips in a heated kiss.

"What are you two whispering about?" he asks, nuzzling his stubble along my neck, his sleep-worn tone creating a tingle all the way to my toes.

His morning wood presses against my stomach, and before I realise it, both Jacob and Nick are awake, the five of us starting the day in the best way we know how: tangled together in the sheets.

***

The car park is quiet when I pull into the coffee shop where Penelope was supposed to be meeting her friend. Anxiety swarms in my belly as I turn off the engine, take a steadying breath, and twiddle the bracelet on my wrist. If anything happens, they can find me.

He said we're safe… Nick, Jacob, Leo, and Wyatt believe it, and I've got this on just in case. The concern swimming in my stomach is nothing more than nerves. It's all going to be totally fine.

With one last look around, I climb out of the car, close the door, and head for the coffee shop. The smell of the rich coffee makes me feel welcomed the second the bell rings above my head, the tension falling from my shoulders in the way only the victorious life juice that is coffee can help with.

When I look around, Ruby's nowhere to be seen. So, making my way to the counter, I order our usual and pick out a table by the window, looking out as I wait. Winter clings on, the low temperatures reminding me just how far away summer really is, but as the sun peeks out through the clouds, hope blossoms.

Maybe there are better things on the horizon.

I'm a million miles away when the drinks are placed on the table, the action jolting me out of the reverie I've found myself in. Outside, a familiar black car pulls up, and Ruby jumps out of it, shrugs her hood over her head, and makes her way to me with a small smile.

It's not quite the over excited jump-and-wave that Tamsin might have got from Mercedes four months ago, but it's one hell of an improvement on where we started.

"You know he could join us now, right?" I ask as she drops into the seat opposite, shrugging off her jacket and leaving it draped over the back of the chair

"Who?"

"Whoever the guy is that drives the car," I reply, wrapping my fingers around the mug and blowing steam over the top.

"Yeah, that won't be happening."

"Why not? I'll bring Leo along, and the two of them can sit and have a catch up, too."

I'm not sure Leo's said in so many words that he knows the guy, and I'm sure the person driving is also the one she was forever checking her phone for, because even that's become less so since that same car has become a regular occurrence.

It's pretty sad for me to have noticed that, but with everything being so up in the air over the last few months, every detail has felt like it might be important, and that extends to the car that brings Ruby, apparently.

"Just because you guys are all important now doesn't mean the rest of us are off the hook," she grumbles under her breath.

Pocketing that snippet of information for later, I change the subject, hoping for at least one positive interaction in all the time we've spent together.

"Did they tell you how much we raised at the event?"

"Not an exact figure, but Amy was doing an excited little dance when we turned up this week, so it must have been plenty." She scoffs, clearly remembering the moment. "But I suppose that means your obligation to me is complete."

The twinge of sadness in her tone surprises me considering how hostile she's been this entire time, but, despite the odds stacked against us, we've managed to forge something of a friendship, no matter how odd that might look to the rest of the world.

"Me?" I ask with a raise of my eyebrows. "You've been trying to shake me off since the very start."

Ruby concedes the point with the tip of her head and another small smile, scooping the cream off her hot chocolate and shoving it in her mouth as we let the quiet fall over us both.

"Yeah, well.. you're all right, I suppose," she eventually admits.

"I don't know how it's supposed to work, but I'm sure there's usually more than just one pair left at the end... but I didn't have any plans to drop you like a hot cake just because our official time is up," I admit.

"I'm not sure I want to continue spending time with you if I'm not going to get anything out of it," she replies, straight-faced for a second, and then once my surprise has finally registered on my face, she barks out a laugh, adding, "Just kidding."

"And what exactly were you getting out of this, anyway?"

Liselle turned up one day and told us that we were joining this programme. No ifs, no buts, no choice. It never occurred to me that the Little Sisters might have been given an option, never mind an incentive.

"Aside from the extra credit on my uni applications and the time out of school?" she asks, sipping the hot chocolate. "Oh, and the threats against my family for not keeping proper tabs on you and your growing harem?"

"What?" I balk.

"I also get regular trips out with you prissy princesses and an additional bursary to *keep up with the trends*," she says with air quotes and a roll of her eyes.

"So, they're paying you to take part?"

As well as threatening her family and giving her some bonuses for any future endeavours. Sure, if she decides to go on to further education, that will be useful, but it's not exactly the be all and end all, and it certainly doesn't override threats.

"I guess," she replies with a shrug. "I mean, no one really needs it. The tuition at South Beach High isn't exactly a walk in the park, so none of the girls who attend there are short of money." *Except me.* She doesn't say it, but that's what she means.

Her style is not exactly mainstream, but it's chosen well, and she's always seemed to have the right thing for each occasion. But as I think on it, she paled at the price of those designer jeans, even though they were already discounted, and the wrap she wore for the spa day still had its sales tag on.

Ruby's been keeping up with the rest of these girls the whole time, sliding in with them and us, doing her best to get information and fit in. No wonder she was grumpy about having to be here.

"But that's all stopped now, hasn't it?" I ask.

"The money, the programme? Yeah."

I shake my head. That's not what I mean, and we both know it.

The five of us have made it through: official members. There's no need for her to be taking information back to anyone now. They said all the surveillance would stop, but her hesitation gives us both pause for thought

"I'm sure it will soon," she brushes off, avoiding my face and looking out the window instead.

There's so much I'd like to tell her.

This was all just some sick kind of game. Tamsin is still alive somewhere. We've made it through, and things can only go up from here. Whoever is holding this over her head will let her off the hook now… but will they?

Instead, I say, "Well, it's all over now… the programme and everything, so I'm sure it will settle down again," hoping that's the truth of the matter.

It's been… interesting getting to know her.

It's not exactly been easy, or even enjoyable at points. In fact, proving to her that I'm more than just some spoilt little rich girl has been down right hard work a lot of the time but worth it. She's blunt, honest, and linked in here somewhere, somehow. Hopefully, one day, she'll become an ally.

"So, how are things?" I ask, changing the subject again, hopefully moving us on to safer ground this time.

"Boring. Revision sucks," she replies grumpily, but it's enough to break the tension, the seriousness of the conversation we were having, and all the things I can't quite explain to her.

She could be involved here, may even be on our side, but The Sect took away Tamsin without a second thought or a backwards glance. I don't want to pull Ruby any further into this dangerous game than I have to. So, for the next half an hour, we talk about school, exams, and she shows me a couple of the designs she's been working on. Designs I can't wait to see her bring to life.

"No news on Penelope?" she asks as we take a step outside, the brisk wind whistling around the almost empty carpark.

"Afraid not. Aimee's funeral is being shared virtually on Wednesday, though. I can send you the link if you're interested?" Not that a virtual funeral is going to be interesting, but… you know.

I was surprised things had moved so quickly, considering the situation surrounding her murder, but we're not exactly in a position to be asking questions. And if laying her to rest quickly is what helps her family to draw a line under this whole thing, then who am I to question it?

"I didn't really know her," she replies with the shake of her head.

Did any of us?

Aimee was the fun one. Happy and smiley. She did the cooking in the pool house most of the time. She welcomed Tamsin and me with open arms and personalised travel mugs, and she always managed to find the good in any given situation. But all that changed when Tamsin *left...*

Not even Aimee could find a silver lining for that. None of us could.

As the Angels were dragged further and further into the game with The Sect, and the losses began to stack up, you could see that happy-go-lucky spirit sinking. Aimee couldn't play the game like Stephanie could, and she wasn't as Jaded about it as Charlotte was, but she was solid, she was my friend, and her loss is being felt greatly.

It didn't come with the shock factor of watching the life drain from Charlotte's body, or the hope that she still might be out there somewhere. I've clung on to that tiny grain of hope for Tamsin for months, and it was worth it, but there can't be any of that for Aimee. Penelope, maybe…

Wherever she is, I hope she's safe.

"Well, this is me," Ruby says when that same black car pulls in as she drags me out of my thoughts.

He doesn't get out and open the door for her. Doesn't park close enough for me to get a good look, either. Just revs the engine and waits.

"Cool. I'll catch you soon. We'll have an end of year party or something at some point. You two should come," I offer, pushing as much excitement as I can into the statement.

"Parties at a place like yours aren't his thing, but we'll do something soon. Promise." She squeezes my hand and winks, turning away to climb into the back of the car.

The guy driving doesn't even glance my way as the two of them take off, leaving me waiting like an idiot out in the cold before their taillights remind me that I could be tucked up safely in the warmth of my own car with the heaters on. Jumping in, I start her up, taking one last longing look at the coffee shop before heading home.

Why didn't Penelope ever come here? If she did, why does nobody remember?

It's like she walked out of our house and just… disappeared. Poof. Gone.

I'm confident not knowing where she is irritates The Sect at least as much as it does me.

SEVENTEEN

Nick

Sweat trickles down my back as the gym door bangs closed, disturbing the rhythmic pounding of my feet against the treadmill. I'm almost back to my pre-run in with The Sect minutes per mile when Leo storms down the stairs, mumbling something undiscernible to himself. Slowing the machine, I walk it out a bit before I step off, rub my face with a towel, and sling it over my shoulder.

Leo barely spares me a glance, striding straight past me and heading for the punching bag. He doesn't bother with gloves, tape, or warming up, just starts sending his fists flying. One after the other, punch after punch landing in the filled material.

After a minute or two of watching him attempt to exorcise his demons, I go over, holding the bag in place before offering him a real body to hit, and an outlet for whatever's bothering him. He's done it for me, plenty of times over the last month or more. It seems to have become our thing.

Grabbing my gloves from the side, I pull them on, securing the Velcro as the two of us climb into the ring, both already warmed up and ready to go.

"What's got your knickers in a twist?" I ask, barely avoiding the fist that comes flying my way.

"Nothing," he clips, swinging again. "I'm fine."

"Looks like it," I reply, landing two shots to his ribs and following up with a side kick he wasn't expecting.

"You know how it is. Just staring our future in the face."

"No luck on the university hunt?"

"Plenty, but what happens when those three or four years are up? You're going to be a fucking judge, Nick. You can't be linked to the enterprise I'm involved in."

His words take me by surprise, my shock only lasting seconds as he comes at me again, more than just his words hitting their mark.

"And Ivy. She wants to psychoanalyse the stars or whatever. That's not going to be a nine-to- five, home to make your dinner kind of job, either, is it? But I wouldn't want her tainted by what I'm going to be wrapped up in. This is going to be a mess. A fucking shit show of epic proportions."

Each word lands in my chest. Each point accentuated by blows that just keep coming until his breaths are panted, and my ears are ringing.

"I'm going to lose you all."

I barely hear his last words, but I can see the heartbreak written on his face. His pain is all too visible, once again.

The two of us have pushed each other to our breaking points without Jacob, needing the pain to remind us that we're alive, and to punish ourselves for not doing more, for it not being enough. And if the scars Jacob will carry for the rest of life are anything to go by, whatever we've done wasn't enough.

Jacob still won't talk about what happened, tell us who

or why. He's shut the whole thing down and put it in a box never to be opened in the darkest, deepest depths of his mind, but it still wakes him up in the night. Still prowls through his dreams and torments him when he's at his weakest. He thinks we don't see it and don't know, but we do. I can feel it like an ache in my core that won't rest or subside, and I have no idea how to make it better for either of us.

"Let's get these exams done, a university selected, and degrees under our belt. Everything else can be dealt with later," I placate, hoping to hell I'm right. "There's no point worrying about tomorrow's problems today."

"Maybe for you, but I've got to prepare for the future, for the worst-case scenario," he argues as I block another dangerous looking kick.

"We'll find a way. Until death, remember?"

It feels like a lifetime ago that the five of us sat in that bedroom upstairs, me bloody and broken, and the four of them desperately trying to cling on to the hope that we could pull through this together. Little did we know when Ivy took that blade and sliced her palm, pressing that cut against matching ones on each of ours as we promised to love, to care for, and to protect each other until death, just exactly how much that would be tested.

Not that any of us would take it back or change anything. I can't imagine my life without Leo's face to punch or Wyatt's calming influence. Without the woman who sets my blood on fire or the literal other half of me. I have no idea what I expected my life to look like, my relationship to become, but it is both intended and completely unexpected to have my twin brother be a part of it.

We're so alike in so many ways, and so completely different in just as many. I guess it stands to reason that it takes three others to manage and complete us.

"And that's been closer than I'd like for more than one of you, too," he replies, snapping me back into the moment.

The two of us fall quiet, trading punches until Leo has chased off all the demons haunting him right now. Until all of his fear is gone. We don't need to name any more, to go over and over it. We've been thrown in a pressure cooker and watched, but now, the power is off, and it's just the five of us simmering away until we're ready to climb out and get on with the rest of our lives.

We just have to realise the heat is off and we're still alive, still breathing, and still together to do it.

"Did Jacob tell you he managed to get hold of Sophie?" I ask, holding the ropes apart for him to climb through. "Family dinner, Pendleton Prep style when she's back. What do you think?"

"I think, just because we've been told any and all surveillance in this house has been turned off or removed does not mean that I trust it has. I'd like to give them the benefit of the doubt, but considering some of the conversations we may need to have with them, I'd be suggesting we dine elsewhere," he replies, testing the split in his lip before reaching for the first aid kit. "Help me with this, will you?"

I pull a couple of the Steri-Strips free from their sealed packet, holding his lip together before placing them carefully along the cut. There's nothing more than our laboured breathing echoing around the room, our sweat cooling against both our bodies as he tapes my brow up, too.

"We'd better get cleaned up," he says, the fear no longer lingering behind his eyes.

"It'll all work out, Leo. Trust me," I say with a wink, gripping the back of his neck for a moment before walking away.

If this had been Ivy, the air would be charged with sexual tension, and I'd have licked the sweat from her brow and plundered her mouth with my tongue. I'd have reminded her exactly what a force I can be when I want something, but Leo and I don't have that kind of relationship. We both want the same things. We just have different ways of going about getting them, and learning to trust each other has been a process—something we're having to choose to do.

"Do you have any suggestions on where to take Sophie and Carlos for dinner?" I ask. "There's no way I can take them back to that horrendous pizza place."

Leo flicks off the lights, and I close the door behind us, the house huge and quiet as we head through the entranceway, up the stairs, through the hall, the second set of stairs, and finally to the room we claimed as our own. All of this space is a little over the top now it's just the five of us, and if there were a way to get this bed somewhere else, we'd totally move it all.

Unfortunately, the suite we chose has everything we could possibly need, apart from a kitchen. It's both a blessing and a curse as I look at the empty mugs on the coffee table while the sound of quiet voices carry from the office.

"Leave it with me," he says, heading for the shower as I follow the sound, resting my shoulder against the doorjamb when I see Ivy and Wyatt sitting in the middle of a pile of open prospectus books.

"Making any progress?" I ask.

"Not really," Ivy admits with a giggle, laughing at something Wyatt pointed out.

"And these places all have courses for everyone?" I ask. "Has Jacob even decided what he wants to go on and study? You know he's only here this year because I practically blackmailed him into it, right?"

It wasn't as bad as that, not really, but he's got no definitive plan, no goal, no direction. And even now that we're embroiled with The Sect, they gave no final decision on the Angels, just that their futures were ours to decide. I suppose that makes sense in the wider scheme of things. That's why there are some Angels who have gone on to create amazing careers for themselves, and others, like our mother, who have found themselves socialites and philanthropists through no choice of their own. Our mother has always seemed to enjoy the spotlight, so maybe that worked out well for her, but I can't imagine that being Ivy's ideal, or Jacob's, for that matter.

They're both destined to go on to bigger and better things than that.

"He hasn't decided yet, no," Wyatt replies, his concerned gaze flicking to mine. "But most of these have what we need, and anything we don't have, they can do virtually."

"Virtually?"

"Yeah, I called my father. Apparently, the world is our oyster," he adds with the shrug of his shoulders.

I guess that certainly opens doors, but Leo has spent

way more time than I think he's willing to admit searching for the perfect place for us all to attend. I know he left this whole stack of suggestions on the desk, but I'd be willing to put money on the fact that he's got a preference.

"Grab your favourites. Show me what you're thinking," I say, dragging a chair over to join them. "Actually, on second thought, I'm going to quickly get washed up. How long until Jacob gets back?"

"Twenty minutes," Ivy replies, looking at the clock behind my head. "Do you need a hand?"

"Always."

My rumble of a reply has Wyatt smirking as Ivy jumps up, closing the distance between us quickly before snatching my hand and dragging me through to the bathroom. Of course, we end up in the one Leo's already making use of, his eyebrows raising as she shimmies her leggings and underwear off, dropping them to the floor, with her soft jumper following just seconds later.

"I thought you were the one who needed to shower," Ivy says, stepping away from me with a smile, her tits bouncing as she moves to the steamy enclosure where I know Leo waits.

I've never lost my clothes so fast in my life, even with the humid air clinging to my sweat-slicked skin doing its best to hold me back. Stalking into the huge enclosure, I find Leo already running his soapy hands over her breasts, her back pressed against his chest as her head rests against his shoulder. Comfortable. Peaceful.

"Does that feel good, sugar?" I ask, turning on another set of shower heads, the ice-cold water doing nothing to quash the fire burning in my veins—the one that only she ignites.

I do my best to quickly wash up, not afraid of getting her dirty, but more than enjoying the sounds she makes as Leo builds her up, his quiet whispered words only adding to whatever crackles in the air.

"So good," she moans, pressing her legs together after his fingers barely graze against where she so clearly wants him to be—wants us to be.

Her lids are heavy, her heated gaze catching mine, drawing me like a moth to a flame as I press my lips against hers. One hand reaches to grip my bicep as I lift her, pressing her tiny body between the two of us as the water washes away the bubbles revealing the sexiest flush covering her skin.

"Did you have something in mind?" I ask, imagining all the filthy things currently playing out behind her eyes. "Want us to fill you up again?"

A shiver of anticipation ripples over her skin as Leo tugs her nipple, and she writhes in my arms

"Anything. Everything."

She's already wet for us when I slide my fingers over her pussy, holding her up with nothing more than one hand and Leo when I line my cock up and drive into her, a groan of pleasure ripping from my chest.

Leo bites down on the soft flesh where her neck meets her shoulder, and rather than stretching her out like I expected, he continues to torture her nipples, tugging and rolling one and then the other while I get lost in the feel of her squeezing tightly around me.

It takes nothing more than minutes for her to come on a moan, our names echoing around the room as we drag every last second of pleasure from her body, with me following her over the edge just moments later.

"I think our boy over here needs a little help," I comment on panted breaths, leaning back against the cold tiles as I lower Ivy back to the floor.

Without a second's hesitation, she drops to her knees, wrapping one hand around the base of him as the other grips his arse, and she slides her hot mouth down his length, working his body until he's thrusting up, gripping her hair, and coming down her throat, finally succumbing to her siren call.

"Fuck, you're beautiful," Leo purrs, gently running the back of his fingers down her cheek.

We set about cleaning up, again, and manage to get dressed and sorted without giving in to more sex, but not before Jacob arrives back, looking between the three of us knowingly.

EIGHTEEN

"**W**here did you find this place again?" Nick asks, looking out of the window as he follows the GPS down yet another country lane.

"Google," Leo replies with a shrug.

"And it definitely exists, right? You checked the street view, and it had reviews… because I can't for the life of me imagine there's a restaurant out here in the middle of bloody nowhere," Nick grumbles.

"The reviews were good, and there's plenty of miles for a village to appear. Quit worrying, and concentrate on not crashing, will you?" Leo says with a roll of his eyes.

I can only be grateful the weather has finally given us some reprieve from the incessant drizzle, rain, drizzle, that's been going on since forever. I'm sure we had winter at some point, but this *springtime* seems to hold lots of rain, and not so many pretty flowers. I can only imagine how much worse this drive would be with rain hammering down, too.

Although, it's not just the size of the huge BMW in the narrowest country lanes known to man that's the issue. It's the nerves and the ego packed into the car vying for position that make it almost unbearable.

"I don't know what you're worrying about, but I can promise you they already love you," Jacob whispers to me whilst Nick and Leo continue to bicker like an old married couple in the front.

"No, it's not that. I'm fine. It's fine," I reply, attempting to brush him off.

This is just the first time we've stepped out together as a group. Officially. Like a couple, only more. And when we met Sophie and Carlos before, it was clear that Leo cared about Jacob, and that I was there for Nick, but the reality is so much more complicated than that, and when we're all together like this, it's obvious. So fucking obvious.

Not that I'm ashamed of them or us—of this thing. We're together. I just don't know how the rest of the world is going to take that, or, more pressingly, what Nick and Jacob's big sister is going to think of the whole thing.

"I thought I'd been doing a pretty good job of taking your mind off the nerves," Wyatt says, squeezing my hand where it rests against his thigh, the three of us pressed together in the back of the car.

"You had," I say, my mind going straight to the orgasms he graced me with this afternoon.

"Had? Maybe you need a reminder of the beautiful, strong, powerful woman you are, then, huh? Maybe it should be me sitting between you and Jacob as the Devil between two Angels."

With a smile, I squeeze his fingers, pushing down the nerves as a small row of shops appear ahead. *This is it.* Nick pulls around the back of the corner plot, and I see the red hanging sign swinging in the breeze.

We quickly make our way to the front door, the black-glass facade opening into a beautiful dining room, with a server already waiting to take us to our seats. My heels click against the black tiles on the floor; the crisp white linens a huge contrast to the darkness everywhere else.

Black marble lines the bar, and the copper hanging lights showcase another beautiful contrast. When Leo pulls out a heavy seat covered with black leather, I realise I've been utterly distracted.

Sophie releases Jacob and hugs Nick quickly before throwing her arms around me as Leo pushes my seat under, almost toppling us all to the floor. We laugh, she smiles, and the seven of us sit.

"This is an improvement on the last place we met," Carlos says, an impressed look covering his olive features. "Hopefully the food matches the décor."

"The reviews were good," Leo repeats with a shrug, brushing it off, despite the nerves I know he's hiding.

But this isn't the first thing he's looked into, found for us, or worked out. His need to know more, to delve deeper is something I've missed up until this point. Although, even when I think back to our first get together, back at the meet and great mixer, he wanted to know more about me, about Tamsin. It seems this isn't something new, it's just a part of who he is.

"Well, it's good to see you with my own eyes," Sophie says, taking Jacob's hand over the table and drawing everyone's attention to the man of the hour.

"Yes, sorry about scaring you all, but it was a little out of my control," Jacob replies with a warm smile.

"Don't worry, we've kept them up to date," Wyatt adds, shaking the bracelets on his wrist.

"I'm not sure I'd have survived in there without your help," Jacob admits. "And that of Leo's contacts." His gaze travels to the man in question—the one sitting between us—before going back to Carlos. "So, thank you, for everything you were able to do."

"It wasn't as much as we wanted, but I'm glad it helped," Carlos replies.

"Wait, what?" I ask, confused.

When we came to them before it was to ask for help to get Jacob out, and that's only happened recently, so what else has been going on?

"We have contacts here, there, and everywhere. It may have taken us until now to find a way to get Jacob in rather than out, but we've been supporting him as best we could from out here," Carlos explains.

Before I have chance to ask any more questions, the waiter appears with wine, filling the glasses and taking our orders. I've barely even glanced at the menu, too distracted by the opulence we're surrounded by and the conversation at hand. After I quickly pick something, he takes the rest of the orders, then quietly disappears again.

"It was actually something Leo's friend suggested," Sophie says, drawing my attention to her. "About making space for Jacob to be in this society rather than out, and whilst your friend was looking for a new start, it seemed like as good an opportunity as any to kill two birds with one stone."

My friend?

"Penelope." The word hangs in the air as conversations continue around us. Sophie winks as a smile pulls up one side of her perfectly-lined lips, waiting for the rest of the pieces to fall in place for me. "Penelope is the thing you took to Italy and have found a home for, not whatever you won at the auction."

"Well, the sculpture has a lovely spot on the side table at Tia's new place, but her assistant is also settling in nicely," Sophie confirms.

"Because with one out of the way there would be a space to be filled, and with Jacob being a bloodline member, and already offering to take a place in the Angels, it would make sense to put him in that place," I think aloud.

"Timing was important," Carlos adds.

"Yes, because of Oliver and Stephanie," I ponder. "And Aimee… you didn't?" I ask, the question trailing off, too afraid to say the worlds.

"Kill her? No," Carlos replies with a disappointed shake of his head.

But is he disappointed I think that of him, or that it happened?

"We were, unsurprisingly, otherwise engaged," Sophie adds.

Yes, taking Penelope far, far away from us and The Sect.

"And she'll be safe?" I ask, pushing past the lump in my throat from thinking about Aimee. "I can't imagine The Sect is likely to just give up a potential member without any kind of comeback."

"Don't worry, we've got that covered," Carlos tells me cryptically, whatever he was going to say next being interrupted by the waiters and our food.

The conversation turns lighter, with Sophie asking Nick about helping her with some design work for an upcoming charity event she's hosting, and we fall into easy discussion about this talent I never knew he had.

I rib him about all those hours I spent messing around trying to get the fundraiser invitations looking something like professional, and Wyatt reminds us all that Nick was the one to do the invitation for the first get together at their place. Not that I knew that or them at that point.

It feels like a lifetime ago.

Carlos orders a round of whiskey as the meal draws to a close, the concern I had swirling in my stomach about how obviously smitten the five of us are clearly a complete waste of time as he tops up Sophie's wineglass, a whole conversation happening between them with nothing but a long, lingering look.

"Before we go, there was something else I wanted to discuss," Carlos states, accepting the glass from the waiter and waiting for him to leave before continuing. "As you're likely aware, Nick, Jacob, and Sophie's father was the link between my family and The Sect. He allowed us to access certain privileges that aren't usually awarded to outsiders. Not least, competitive rates and personal support from your family," he says, looking at Leo. "As you can imagine, we have taken considerable risks with securing Jacob a space in your final lineup. Not that I wouldn't have done anything for Sophie, but we have a request." He sips his drink, the ice clinking around the glass as he holds us all captive.

"You want an in," Wyatt determines.

"We would like to continue the work we're doing in London, and some of that is going to require the ongoing support of The Sect, specifically Leo's father, Vincent. It would be appreciated if you could find space for Jacob to work alongside you, and for him to be our point of contact."

I don't think stunned silence is the reply he was expecting or looking for as he cooly waits us out.

"So, he doesn't get a say in this?" Nick spits the words out, breaking the awkward moment by throwing his arm out to gesture to his brother as he stands, shoving his chair back, the scraping drawing more than one set of eyes our way.

Carlos is silent when I place my hand on Nick's forearm, some of the fury currently rushing through his body simmering down at my touch. Wyatt pulls Nick's chair back into place, pushing gently against his shoulders as we all wait for him to sit and the rest of the room to go back to their previous conversations.

"We are likely heading to university in September," Leo explains calmly, his fury sheathed beneath the twitch of his fingers on the glass. "I know we've officially missed the cut off for standard enrolment, but that doesn't seem to be too much of a problem for our new connections. I will be taking over from my father at some point in the future, but no date has been set yet."

There's not so much of a twitch of irritation from Carlos's cold, blank exterior as he sips the whiskey in his glass, waiting for more.

"I can't see why my father would go back on any

agreement you have in place," Leo says with a tip of his head, ignoring the way Nick's anger still vibrates through him.

"This is bullshit," Nick throws out, clearly not done. "How the hell can you sit there and condone taking his choice away?" he asks, looking at Sophie, pleading for understanding from his sibling.

"It's cute that you think any of us have had a choice in where we've ended up and what we're doing," she replies coldly, a long way from the smiling, gentle woman that has been with us all evening. This version of her I can imagine being the fiancée of a mafia boss.

The flip of that switch is scary. Impressive, but scary.

Is this what it takes to hold your own in this male dominated world?

"She's right," Wyatt says, and my gaze snaps to his, even as he holds the cold and distant look Sophie sends his way. "Our lives here have been predetermined by The Sect. If doing this got Jacob out and safe, then so be it."

"You don't think he's been through enough?" Nick asks, incredulity wrapped around each word.

The separation. The nightmares. The scars.

He's not the same as he was before his time with The Sect. But none of us are.

"You don't get to decide this. None of us do," I say, slicing through the tension and looking over to the only person who can make this decision. "Jacob?"

If I thought the table was tense before, I was wrong.

All eyes fall to the man on my left, with only Leo separating the two of us at the large, round table. Silent.

Still.

Jacob's hands clench and release around the glass, his gaze lowered to the tablecloth as all eyes rest on him.

"I'm sorry. I can't do this," he declares before pushing his seat back and walking away.

Nick tries to follow him, but without even turning to acknowledge the movement, Jacob waves him away, keeping his head down as he crosses the restaurant and walks out of the door, the bell tinkling above lost beneath the softly playing music.

"Maybe I could…" Leo offers, looking forlornly at the door.

"This is your suggestion. Why don't you go and explain yourself to him?" Nick grumbles, glowering at Sophie.

"Just give the guy a minute," Wyatt intervenes, acutely aware of how Nick gets with Jacob out of sight. His irritation will only build until Jacob returns, the constant state of panic doing none of us any good.

It will just take time. Our systems have been flooded with stressors for weeks and months, and some of the things we've endured will live on with us long after the flight or fight response has calmed down. Therapy is what we need, but who exactly can be trusted with the knowledge of kidnap and murder?

I may be putting some of my more recently acquired counselling skills to use sooner than anticipated, and on people closer to me than I'd have liked, but the only way we're going to be able to heal and move on from the trauma we've been through is to process it properly. And whilst knocking the shit out of each other has taken the edge off, it's clear that both Nick and Leo are holding on to more than they ought to be.

"May I?" I ask, gesturing to the doorway.

The conversation around the table has all but died, any good feelings from Jacob being returned safely now drowned out by the mafia request.

"You've got ten minutes and then I'm coming to find you both," Wyatt says decidedly.

"No problem," I agree, plucking my jacket from the hostess before I leave.

The darkness of the evening wraps around me when I step outside, but at least the rain hasn't made a reappearance as I seek out Jacob on the empty street. There's nothing but fields for miles outside of the half a dozen shops nestled together. A butcher, a baker, a mini supermarket, and some kind of clothing shop with heavy shutters that calls to me as I head away from the restaurant, looking for the man of the hour, but he's nowhere to be seen.

"I honestly thought they'd send Leo," Jacob says from somewhere behind me, making me jump.

Whirling around, I clasp my chest, my heart beating madly as he scares the living shit out of me. Relief mingles with fear, and it's something that reflects in his eyes as he steps forward into the light, pulling out of his hiding spot as he shoves his hands deep into his pockets.

"Jeez, you scared me half to death," I comment, still attempting to get my breathing under control.

"Sorry," he replies, shrugging his shoulders, despondency radiating from him as he crosses the road towards me, bumping his shoulder against mine. "You okay?"

"I'm good." I nod, and the two of us start slowly meandering, moving with no destination in mind. Just needing the action to keep us grounded.

"This isn't exactly what I imagined when we were told that The Sect were the greatest force in the world," he admits. "Tagging along with my boyfriend so that my future brother-in-law can keep hold of a connection to discounted prices is a world away from where I thought I'd end up."

"Where did you see yourself?" I ask, conscious he's been quiet about the whole thing since he returned to us. Long gone is the easy breezy version of him that we met back at the beginning.

"Recently? Six feet under, but even that was a pipe dream." He scoffs out a depreciating laugh before continuing. "I've never had a goal or a dream. Not like Nick. He always wanted to be the one in charge, making decisions, changing lives. Law is where his heart is, and he'll make an amazing judge, if only he can keep his emotions in check when it comes to the hard things."

He falls quiet, thinking, and as we get to the end of the tiny road, he turns, leaning his forearms against the damp stone wall and looking out over the empty fields.

"I'm only here because you guys broke the rules. I shouldn't get a say or a decision about who I am or what I do. I should be the waif The Sect were moulding me into— the man seen but not heard. Silent and steady. I can't do anything for you all out here."

My heart breaks for him, for the vulnerability he's allowing me to see, even as he's turned away from me.

Wrapping my arms around his waist, I press my chest to his back, my cheek against his shoulder blade, and wait, hoping to absorb some of his pain.

"And here I was thinking we'd made it more than clear just how integral to us you are," I tell him quietly.

"You have, it's just…" He trails off with a sigh.

"You don't have to do this. Leo can speak with his father, and we can find another way. What's the worst thing Carlos can do? Bring Penelope back?" I scoff. "I have a feeling that Mr Mafia has a soft spot for women, and there's no chance he's sending one back to certain death. Oh, that is, if he could extricate her from the grips of both his and your sisters. I think not. What is it you want Jacob? What do you feel like you're missing?"

Silence stretches out around us, a brisk breeze blowing over the field and cutting around his broad back. Eventually, Jacob sighs again before turning around and wrapping me in his warm embrace.

"I want you all to be happy," he admits.

My heart squeezes at his words. This selfless, beautiful man has given himself time and time again, and the only thing his heart desires is the happiness and peace of those he loves.

"I've never had a big dream, I only even hoped to help Nick with his, but now my circle is so much bigger than that. How will I be able to love and support you all? How can I ever be enough?" The last question is muttered into my hair as he presses a kiss to my head, and I almost miss it. Almost.

Turning, I place my hands on his cheeks, dragging his

gaze to mine as he holds me close. Safe. Secure. Intimate.

"I don't know what they did or what they said to you whilst you were gone, but if you ever need to talk, I'm here."

He nods, the amber in his hazel gaze burning bright under the streetlights.

"What I do know is that we are a team. Together. Until death. Or do you want to go back on your word?"

Anger flashes through his expressive gaze before he violently shakes his head.

"Good. Now, a little secret. Something to keep between you and me, because those three sure as hell can't take it." I swallow the lump of emotion threatening to clog my throat and forge on. "None of us are enough. Not on our own. There's a reason we're together the way we are, and it's because we need each other. One person will never be able to take away from the four of you."

His gaze softens, his hands squeezing my waist as he holds me and absorbs the raw truth spilling from my lips.

"Happiness is the life we are going to create together, in time. I know you want to be a part of that, no matter how you feel about your time away from us. We could never be whole without you."

A tear slips over the edge of his lashes as he closes his eyes, and he inhales a shuddering breath before pressing his lips together.

He's beautiful. He's perfect. And he's ours.

Nobody is going to take him from us again, and nobody is going to demand anything from him, either. He chooses his path, but he's going to do it knowing he's not alone in this world. Not now, and not ever again.

"Thank you," he whispers, reaching up to brush away the errant tears.

"Now, knowing that we're with you no matter what, do you want to go with Leo when he takes over from his father? Are you willing to find yourself a place in their organisation that will bring you peace and joy? And will you use that connection to strengthen the ties between us and your sister's family?"

"Well, when you put it like that…"

"You can say no and find your joy elsewhere. Work with me, or Wyatt, support Nick if you really want to… or find something that is completely your own, but I'm not sure alone is what you really want."

It never has been. The only thing he wanted was to support Nick, then to love us. Taking him away drove a wedge between us I wasn't sure we'd be able to repair. Luckily for us, our love is more resilient than that.

"I'll find a place with Leo. I'll be their link," he agrees, a small smile tipping up one corner of his mouth. "Someone's going to need to keep an eye on him, anyway, and make sure he's not going rogue."

"Who better to keep him in line than the man who holds his heart in his hands, huh?" I ask, returning the smile as I let my hands fall from his face to hang over his shoulders.

"Oh, I'm not the only one that holds that beaten and battered up thing, and you damn well know it," Jacob replies, pulling me into his chest and wrapping his arms around my back. "I think we're needed."

Turning, I catch Nick's worried gaze as he loiters under the lights from the restaurant, flicking his collar up before calling over. "You two done yet? It's fucking freezing."

We both manage a smile, one last quick squeeze, and then we intertwine our fingers and head back. I don't know about Jacob, but I feel one hell of a lot lighter for finally being able to get all that off my chest.

"You good?" Nick asks, puling Jacob in for a man hug, back-slap type thing, the two of them pressing their foreheads together as they breathe simultaneously, just for a second. "You know you don't have to do this, right?"

"I know. I'm good," Jacob replies. "Let's get this sorted out and put to bed."

Jacob pulls away, pushing back through the doorway and into the restaurant as Nick and I follow, all eyes at the table turning to take us in as we stride across the room and sit down, any conversations they were previously having forgotten.

"I'll do it," Jacob announces.

NINETEEN

Nick

The sound of my footsteps is eaten up by the plush carpet, the silence of the first floor a reminder of everything and everyone we've been through to get here. Weeks and months of stress, trauma and worrying, and now we're left with a huge house and an even bigger expectation. It shouldn't have come as much of a surprise, I suppose.

I should have known this was coming.

I thought this was a way out. An escape from the wretched gaze of our mother. I thought this would be freedom.

I should have known better.

Instead, I heard the words power and wealth and equated that with something it wasn't: an escape.

I should have listened.

They told us at the very beginning that our lives had been mapped, our paths chosen. Why I ever believed that we had a choice in this, I don't know.

I guess it's too late.

At least this is a future geared towards our strengths and towards the things we want to do rather than whatever position Francesca Barrett would have pushed Jacob and I towards, but still… it's not what any of us would have chosen necessarily.

The hour in the gym has barely take the edge off my irritation; Carlos's demand still ping-ponging around the inside of my skull. When the bedroom door bangs back against the wall, pushing open easier than I expected, four sets of confused eyes fall straight to me.

"Nice to see you're in a better mood," Leo grumbles, turning his back to me again.

"It's not the same without your face to pound."

"Hey, I offered," Wyatt intervenes, like I'd ever consider going full throttle in his direction.

"I think we've got it down to two," Ivy says with a smile, ignoring the bickering and calling me over.

"All of the ones Leo picked out have my classes. I really don't care where we go as long as we're together," I reply, sick of going around in circles about which university to go to.

The courses will be the same, and as long as we're all going to be there, I really, honestly, truly, could not care less about anything else. I don't know why they don't get that.

"This one is farther along the coast, so Wyatt can teach you how to surf," Ivy starts, pushing a brochure into my hand as I drop onto the floor beside her, looking over the mess they've made on the coffee table.

"If we're going to be taking over from mine and Wyatt's father in the future, this is the last chance we're going to get to choose where we want to be, but this one is closer to home for both of you," Leo says, looking at Jacob and me.

"So, close to home or by the sea?" I ask, holding them up one at a time.

"Yep," Wyatt agrees with a nod, leaning forward to rest

his elbows on his knees.

"Sea. There's fuck all left for us at The Manor," I decide easily. It was barely more than a mausoleum when we left.

"Told you." Jacob grins triumphantly.

"I thought you might have wanted to be closer to home with everything Sophie's done to help us out recently, and to support your mother," Ivy explains with the shrug of her shoulders.

"Sophie moved into a place in London with Carlos a while ago, although I don't think it was official. She made up something about how it's easier to get to the office, but she managed just fine for years before that. I'm reasonably sure she only stayed to keep an eye on us," I add, smiling at Jacob.

She may be demanding things I don't want Jacob to have to give right now, but after her instant change in demeanour last night, it's clear to see that we don't know our big sister quite as well as we thought we did. There's a whole other side to her we haven't been privy to until now.

"Probably," Jacob agrees. "To be fair, no one else was."

"Oh, I dunno," I ponder, thinking about how Andrew somehow always knew where we were, and when we were about to cause some kind of mischief. "And speaking of things we didn't know, Ivy, is your dad the deputy mayor?"

It took me a lot longer than it should have to work out where I'd heard that name before, but the second I placed it, so many things made sense.

"He is, why?" she asks, tugging one foot under the other.

"Because Deputy Mayor Collins is a member of The

Sect. He's been here, in the house, and at our challenges," I explain.

"Oh, yeah," Wyatt says, clicking his fingers, recognition flaring across his face. "He was at the puzzle thing that night."

"And when we were all dragged out of bed after the mixer," Jacob adds.

"When George got his leg broken," Leo explains.

"No...." Ivy says, looking from me to Leo, to Jacob, and then finally holding Wyatt's gaze, the cogs turning behind her eyes. "He's not... He didn't... He wouldn't... Would he?"

"Sorry, baby girl. It looks like he did," Wyatt says, clearly having put the pieces together, too. "You didn't end up in the pool house by accident. You and Tamsin were placed there intentionally by your father."

"Which means he knew what would happen to Tamsin if she didn't pick one of you four... what would happen to me, too. And he knew what was going on when I went home at Christmas, as well as what would happen at New Year's."

"I don't know how much involvement he'd have, because our fathers have been kept completely in the dark," Leo argues. "But if he's been at our challenges, then he had to know something. And if he's been through this process himself, which he must have, then he damn well knew what would happen if Tamsin or you didn't end up with one of us."

"So, not happy with me refusing Spencer's sleazy advances, he packs me off to this place, hoping that I'll pick one of you while knowing that even if I don't, he still controls my future. Is that what you're telling me?" she asks, seething.

"Looks that way," Jacob agrees.

"And, of course, I've played straight into his hands and picked the four of you. All of you. All the men he wanted me to find a place with, I have," she continues, standing and starting to pace as the four of us watch her begin to unravel.

At least we knew we were lambs being led to slaughter.

"I knew there was more to this when he suggested it. No, when *demanded* it." Her lips purse, and her eyes narrow as the last twelve months play out behind her eyes, her irritation only growing. "Fuck," she whispers, defeated.

"Angel, did you choose Nick because you were told to?" Leo asks, ignoring the rest of us as he steps towards her, halting her frantic steps as he takes her hands and catches her attention before repeating his question.

"No," she replies honestly, quickly, her gaze flicking to mine before returning to his.

"And Wyatt? Did anyone tell you to fall for him?"

"Of course not. But he sent me here for you, and I came, and I fell, and I did exactly what I was supposed to," she replies, her words breaking as hurt pours from her.

"Would you rather be without us?" I ask, already knowing the answer.

"Don't be ridiculous," she quips.

"The alternative to *not* picking one of them isn't great, either…" Jacob says, only adding to the tension in the room.

"I know, and as a member, he'd still be in control of my future," she says, her gaze softening as she looks at Jacob.

"Let's get something else straight, then, shall we?" Jacob

asks with the cock of an eyebrow. "Love isn't something you're forced into, it's something you choose, and no matter how you feel about *why* you're here, I know you want to be with us. We wouldn't be whole without you," he declares.

I can't say I've ever witnessed it before, but Ivy practically melts right before our eyes. All the anger that was building just tumbles from her as she steps away from Leo, climbs into my brother's lap, and presses a kiss to his lips.

"Maybe I'll flaunt my newfound boyfriends off at his next event and see just how well his plan to control my life worked out for him," she says mischievously.

"Boyfriends, huh?" Wyatt asks with a smirk, leaning back in the chair, the tension that was crackling around the room just moments ago effectively diffused.

"Erm, I mean… I just thought that was the closest description," Ivy says, stumbling over her words, a blush rising on her cheeks.

"It's cool, sugar. We can be your boyfriends," I say, climbing up from the floor. "But now that we've got that worked out, I'm gonna hit the shower. Are we all good here?"

"We're good," she says, jumping up and gathering the no-longer-required books and booklets from the table before dumping them into the closest bin. "University picked. We're almost out of here, boys."

What was supposed to be a quick kiss as I pass her on my way to the shower turns hot faster than I anticipated, her tongue tangling with mine as she pushes up onto her tiptoes, pulling me in by my shirt.

"To be continued," I say breathlessly. "Let me get cleaned up and then I'll gladly dirty you right up."

"Don't worry. We've got her," Wyatt says, stepping up behind her and pulling her pliant body into his arms. "If you're quick, we might even let you join in," he adds cockily.

Challenge accepted.

Stepping away from them is harder than I thought it would be, my dick definitely having other ideas as I strip off on the way, turn on the shower heads, and throw my clothes in the wash basket. It's probably the quickest shower I've ever taken, and I'm still half expecting one or more of them to come and join me as I turn off the water and reach for the nearest towel, brushing it quickly over my arms and shoulders before tying it around my waist.

Grabbing another towel, I reach for the door, stepping out and rubbing roughly at my hair as I look for them at the sofas. Part of me expects them to be sitting watching a film, with no clue what I'm talking about, but as a moan of pleasure hits my ears, I turn and find the four of them tangled up in the sheets of our huge bed.

"I have no idea who designed this or how the hell they got it in here, but I really don't care," I mutter to myself. This bed is amazing, and we're going to need one when we move.

Leo is laid out on the end of the bed, his feet firmly planted on the floor with Jacob laid crossways, drawing long teasing strokes of his tongue up and down the length of his thick cock, but it's Ivy who draws my attention.

Her thick, dark locks are pulled back, held tightly in

Wyatt's fist as he rests his back against the headboard, bobbing her up and down his dick, with Ivy sucking and slurping in the dirtiest blowjob I've ever seen. He barely gives her a second to gather her breath before plunging her back down on both himself *and* Leo's face buried beneath her as she rides his tongue.

"Good to know you didn't wait for me."

The semi I'd managed to push away is back with vengeance, tenting the towel as water drips down my chest, gathering in the material as it strains to stay together.

"If you're serious about university and setting up your own practice, we really should be talking about contraceptives," I comment, my brain conjuring up the image of Wyatt pushing our come back inside her just days ago, wishing we could do it again soon. "I'm all in for having you barefoot and pregnant, but if you have things to do first, we really need to do something-"

"She's on the pill," Leo says, cutting me off and pulling back to sink two digits into her wet heat.

"And that's going to be enough, is it?" I ask, gripping myself through the soft fabric.

"Ivy, you want us to wrap it up?" Wyatt asks, but it's like she doesn't even hear us, too lost to sensation until his tone drops, a growl reverberating from his chest as he pulls her back, repeating the question.

"No," she replies, panting and reaching for him.

"Maybe we should talk about this when you're not sex drunk," I suggest, more than ready to join in.

Her blown pupils lock with mine. "Don't tell me what I want," she argues.

There she is: the fighter I was beginning to worry was going soft on us. Not that there's anything wrong with softness, but there's something about the way she argues with me over everything that gets me harder than fucking steel.

"If the girl wants fucking until she can't walk straight, then filling full of come, who exactly are you to tell her otherwise?" Jacob argues. "Stop trying to be a gentleman. It doesn't suit you."

With a shrug, I drop the towel, pluck her from their clutches, and join in, more than ready to let my little fighter take whatever she needs.

TWENTY

Ivy

"**I** feel like we need some kind of celebration," I say, closing my books.

I must have missed half the lecture, my mind wandering to all the things we've been through this year and all the things that are yet to come.

"Celebration?" Leo asks, taking my bag.

"Yeah, but also, no. We've come so far since the start of the year. That's the kind of thing to be celebrated, but we've also lost so many people. Don't you think it would be strange without the girls and everyone?"

"We had the big *get to know you* party at the start of the year, and then you did that dramatic *keep your paws off my man* demonstration outside the administration buildings. I'm reasonably sure nothing could be weirder than that."

"I mean, you say that, but…" I let the sentence trail off. We both know there have been plenty of things weirder than that to happen this year.

The two of us file out, following the handful of people down the corridor.

"Mostly people have left in ones and twos. I'm not sure

it's really as obvious as it feels. I've never been asked about it, so something credible must have been explained. Or maybe you're right and a night showing everyone we're here might be a good idea," he replies. "But if your ex doesn't fuck off from our heels, he's going to have a problem."

I hadn't even realised that's who was walking behind us until I turn to glower at Spencer, only for his wide, panicked eyes to catch mine, and his steps to falter and slow.

"How did you…?"

"Don't ask," Leo replies, his sad smile holding a whole bunch of pain I really wish it didn't. "Why don't we do a last-minute celebration of life for Aimee? I know you already got to attend the virtual funeral, but she had other friends here, and it would be a good way to celebrate the end of something."

"That sounds like a great idea. Do you think Findlay and Matthew would cater if I asked?"

"Probably." He shrugs, throwing whatever dangerous memories were swirling behind his eyes just moments ago off like they never even existed. "They both loved having Aimee in the kitchen and, as much as I'm sure they're supposed to be watchful and silent, they definitely took a shine to her," he says as we get to the open entrance, where Nick is waiting by the glass doors.

"I'll ask Nick about invitations and then, if it's okay with you all, we can do it at the weekend?"

"Sounds like a plan. I'll mention it to Wyatt when I get back to the house."

"Is everything okay?" Nick asks, looking between us as I realise how secretive we currently look.

"All good. I'll let our girl fill you in whilst I have a chat with Ivy's old friend over there," Leo says, gesturing to Spencer, who finally catches up with us. "Have fun."

"Be nice," I call after him, but he waves me off, paying my words no attention.

"I'm not sure he knows the meaning of the word," Nick replies with a grumble. "Shall we?"

He throws my bag over his shoulder and holds the door for me before the two of us head to our next class. I fill him in on my conversation with Leo, and he agrees to design the invitations, too. It's nothing more than a ten-minute job for him that would likely take me hours.

We're just talking through ideas when the professor bumbles through the doorway, a pile of books in hand, and calls us to order, our conversation being put on hold.

***

"Was this supposed to be a small intimate gathering or…" Wyatt asks, his question trailing off.

"I don't think we know how to do small and intimate," I reply with a smirk.

"Good point. Did you manage to get the info through to the Little Sisters? Are they coming together?" he asks, pining what I'm hoping is the last of Aimee's pictures on the wall.

"Yeah, Ruby passed the message on, but they're not coming together. She wouldn't be caught dead with them was the phrase she used." I can still picture the look of horror on her face when I suggested it. "Do you think we've got enough flowers to hand out?"

"More than enough," Wyatt placates, looking at the buckets lined up before smoothing his hands down my arms and catching my gaze, drawing the worry from my very skin.

"You know how these parties get. There could be a hundred pissed up bodies, with no clue why they're here by the end of the night."

"Then, we'll give them out earlier. There's nothing to say we have to hand them out at the end of the night, and if people choose to leave them here in remembrance, so what?"

"Yeah, I know. I just—"

"Worry?" he says, cutting me off. "There's no need to. We've got this, remember?"

"Thank you."

I can't find the right words to explain just how much it means for him to take my concerns, my worries, and turn them into nothing. He doesn't dismiss them and make me feel like they're less important than they are. He just has this way to remind me how much *more* we are together. More than any worry or concern ever could be.

A bang in the kitchen breaks the moment, making me jump, but as always, Wyatt knows just what to say to calm my racing heart.

"Go grab a drink. We should have guests arriving shortly." He winks, a mischievous smile playing on his face as he ushers me away seconds before the doorbell rings and he greets the first arrivals.

Barely an hour later, and the house is full of people,

laughing and joking, sharing stories from their time with Aimee and hazarding a guess at what and where her pictures were taken. Unsurprisingly, there are some wild theories, but knowing her like I did, I imagine the reality was a touch tamer.

For the first time, it's nice to see the guys actually relaxing. Now that we're official members, the drink limit is lifted, and the cleaners will be along in the morning to turn the house back around. Not that it stops Leo collecting up a couple of empty glasses on his way to the kitchen.

Nick and Jacob loiter at the bottom of the stairs, talking quietly, but keeping an eye on everything and everyone, and last time I saw Wyatt, he was deep in conversation with some guy in the corner of the den. It's weird being here and doing this without the girls.

Sure, at all the other parties, the guys have been front and centre, but there's always been reassurance in the fact that I wasn't alone, the girls were here, and they had my back. Now, it's just me and them—not that I've found myself without one of them near all evening.

Just when I think I can grab five minutes of peace in the fresh air, Ruby cuts off my path to the glass doors, finally making herself known.

"Glad you could make it," I say, noting the deep red blouse she's wearing and the rainbow clips in her hair. "Didn't have you down as a rainbow girl."

"Mercedes said I couldn't come to a celebration for Aimee without something colourful, and apparently a red top doesn't cut it," she replies with a dramatic roll of her eyes. "I thought I'd done really well, but apparently not."

"You look great."

The chiffon blouse sits loosely over her shoulders, with the front tucked into black jeans, and her studded belt matching the back of her heels. It's not exactly rainbows and butterflies, but the colour counts, and it's clear she's made an effort. It's not black on black, so that's progress, and something Aimee would have appreciated.

"Thanks. You, too. Where did you get the pictures from?" she asks, looking past me at the closest one.

"We raided her social media. I have to say, some of the theories about what she's getting up to in them have been pretty amusing," I whisper conspiratorially.

"Yeah, I can imagine."

"You decided against bringing the boyfriend again I see."

"He's not my boyfriend," she counters. "But yours seem to be kicking around." She smirks, raising an eyebrow when she sees Nick's fingers trailing along my lower back as he passes us, silently checking in.

"They are," I agree, watching his sexy arse strutting away, spotting Jacob joining us and resting back against the wall.

"Nick's going to gather everyone together, so you can do the thing before everyone gets too many drinks down them, is that okay?" he asks after saying hey to Ruby.

"Sure," I reply, nerves fluttering n my belly.

"I'll, erm—" Ruby starts, attempting to side-step away.

"Nah, stick with us kid," Jacob cuts her off, halting her in her tracks.

You can see the battle in her eyes. She wants to flee from

the gathering of people about to arrive and the attention that's going to be on me, but she's also not willing to push past Jacob.

People begin to tumble out of each of the rooms, with Nick following from the movie room, Wyatt the den, and Leo ushering everyone out of the dining room before heading back into the kitchen, his head down.

I don't have time to think about that before Jacob hits the wall twice, pushing me forward as all eyes land on me.

"Good evening, everyone, and thank you for joining us to remember and celebrate our good friend Aimee Warren," I begin, taking a sip of my dink to quench the thirst that's suddenly appeared. "I hope you all enjoy a look into her life," I say gesturing to one of the pictures. "And please, do share your happy memories in the remembrance book, which we've left in the den. I'll be sending that on to her family next week."

More than one glass rises in acknowledgement as I take a fortifying breath in before forging ahead.

"You may not have known this about her, but Aimee's favourite flowers were peonies." I smile, looking at the huge things on the sideboard, thinking back to the discussion she had with Tamsin about how they'd be the perfect wedding flower.

"They represent happiness, romance, prosperity, and good fortune, amongst other things, and whilst she can't partake in those things anymore, we thought it would be a nice tribute for you all to take a little reminder of her with you tonight."

"They'll be here all evening. So, whenever you're

ready to head back to your homes and apartments, please help yourself to a stem or two," Jacob adds, gesturing to the flowers, also.

"Hopefully, these happy buds will bring good things your way," I say, raising my glass.

"Good things," Leo echoes back, raising his glass to join mine as the rest of the group follows suit.

"Now, the last thing she'd have wanted in her memory is sadness. So, if someone could turn up that music, there's a dance floor in the dining room, and I know Aimee would have been the first one on it," Wyatt says from the doorway.

And because the DJ was clearly listening in, Aimee's favourite song plays over the speakers, making emotion clog my throat and tears threaten to fall, until Ruby offers her hand out to me. My surprise must be clear, but she just smiles and shrugs, reaching for me and taking us to the proclaimed dance floor.

Not only are we the centre of attention, but we've barely had a drink yet, and the dance floor is empty.

Aimee would have loved this.

Losing myself in the melody, I let Ruby's smile remind me that, even though Tamsin is safe but elsewhere, and the girl friends I'd made here are lost—or were never my friend in the first place—that doesn't mean that there aren't other women around willing to step out of their comfort zones. I'm not the only woman standing in the middle of this male dominated world trying to make her way.

And as more of Aimee's friends, classmates, and the rest of the Little Sisters join us, I finally start to feel the relief I thought I would for getting to the end of this thing.

TWENTY-ONE

Leo

"I'll kick everyone in from outside," I mention to Jacob, ready for this party to be over.

He nods, waving me off as he continues his conversation with one of the guys from his history class. He's missed a lot whilst being under the control of The Sect, and he really needs all the help he can get at this point. So, I leave them to it, slipping out of the glass doors and into the back garden.

The lights are on around the pool, but luckily, no one decided to go for a mid-February dip. That's too cold even for me. There are, however, a few couples cosied up on the decking, keeping warm under the overhead heaters and soaking up a little bit of the quiet evening.

How sad for them that I've come to ruin it all.

After rounding them all up and sending them inside, either to join the rest of the party or to grab a flower and fuck off—I couldn't care either way—I drop down into one of the swinging benches, letting the motion sensors go dark over the other side before pulling out the pack of cigarettes and fishing around in my pocket for a lighter.

If I'd not caught him loitering in the darkness earlier on, I might have jumped when the Zippo lands in my lap—Dex's signature one.

"Thanks, man," I grumble, lighting the stick of poison and drawing the nicotine deep into my lungs before watching it plume out to the heavens, then offering the lighter back to him.

To my surprise, he joins me, stashing the lighter back in the safety of his inside pocket.

"You could have come in, you know? It's all over now. I'm officially a member."

"I'm risking enough sitting out here as it is," he grumbles ominously. "Congratulations on that, by the way."

"Thanks, I think."

"You'll be taking over at some point?"

I nod.

"Is Blaise gonna be your second in command?"

Again, I nod, letting the poison fill my lungs as he asks the questions we both already know the answers to, hesitating over the ones we don't.

"What about your girl?"

Isn't that the million-dollar question?

It's been hard enough work nailing down a university for the next few years that would cater for all of us. We're not going to be able to continue on together after that. Not really.

A judge, a CEO, a psychiatrist, and an underground mob boss. Sounds like the start of a bar joke if you ask me.

"I need to find a position for Jacob. Something that plays to his strengths and that he's going to enjoy. He's going to be our link with La Famiglia," I say, ignoring his question.

"Well, when you're in charge you can set up what you want."

"Yeah, but that will go much smoother if I've got backing for it."

"Maybe in the past you might have needed that," he counters. "Now, you've got all the backing you need, and no one standing in your way."

"What does that mean?" I ask, the hairs on the back of my neck standing up.

As far as I'm aware, there's never been anyone standing in my way. My father wouldn't have allowed it. He may treat me like shit a lot of the time, but that's nothing compared to how he is with other people.

"You got the girl you wanted, you got the guy you wanted back, and there are no arguments about pairing up the finalists." He ticks them off on his fingers like a checklist.

Two of those things are because Aimee died. Here. Stabbed by someone who knew just how to do it, quickly and quietly, who had the knowledge of the campus layout, and the blind spots in the cameras. Murdered by a pro. We just never know who, or why. I guess now, I do.

"Now you and the rest of your merry band don't have to be tied to anyone else. You're free to be whoever you want to be," he adds quietly.

I don't agree with the method, but I understand the logic. Coming from where we do, I get why removing her that way would be his go-to. It's also a relief to know there isn't someone out there seeking to hurt initiates or get on the wrong side of The Sect. No one coming after the rest of us.

"You know they're looking into it, don't you?"

I can only imagine the things The Sect will do to the person that killed one of their potential members, bloodline or bought in, and none of it will be good.

"Good luck to them."

The tip of my cigarette crackles in the silence as I pull another lungful in, relishing the burn before pushing it back to the stars, watching it feather out, then disappear.

"Are you guys good… safe?" I ask.

The threat over their lives still hangs over my head. I know my father would do it, too, if only to keep me in line. But I guess things are happening, changing. It's official. He'll be stepping down, and I'll be stepping up. Pissing me off in the run up to that would be a mistake, although my father hasn't always been known for his rational thought process.

"Yeah, we're good. Josiah has Blaise working closely with him still. He comes home exhausted and closed off. More so than before…"

I nod, getting it.

"I'm on another task closer to home," he says, his gaze flicking to the house so briefly that I'd have missed it if I'd blinked.

"Babysitting?"

"Something like that," he grumbles, clearly not in the mood to talk about it.

"Well, if you ever get an hour spare, or she's coming over to meet Ivy, don't be a stranger, yeah? It's been too long since I kicked your arse on video games."

"Kicked *my* arse? You're off your fucking head." He

barks out an amused laugh, standing as I put out my smoke. "I'll see you around."

"See you soon," I say, pulling him in to slap my hand down against his back.

It's been too long without him, without them both, and as much as being part of Pendleton Prep and The Sect has given me Jacob and Ivy, Nick and Wyatt, I've lost something, too. Not completely, because they'll always be my brothers in all the ways apart from blood, but it's different now. Lines have been drawn, and we've ended up on different sides, kind of.

"Oh, and you're welcome, by the way," he adds quietly, slinking back into the darkness like the shadow he often is.

I'm not sure I'm exactly thanking him for murdering my friend, Ivy's friend, but it sure is nice not to have that problem to solve.

With a loaded sigh, I heave myself from the chair and head back into the noise of the party—the one celebrating the life of said murdered friend.

***

The house is quiet as I tiptoe up the stairs, sweat sticking to my brow as I close the door to the gym behind me and make my way to the kitchen, where the smell of freshly brewed coffee makes it clear I'm not the only one up and moving this early.

Sleep hasn't ever come easily to me, and the habits formed over the last six or more months with The Sect breathing down our necks are going to be hard to come out of. None of us overindulged in alcohol last night, and, despite knowing a cleaning team will be here shortly, the thick of the tidying up is already done.

The house is back to its pre-party state, even if it's not perfect.

Surprisingly, Wyatt is perched at the breakfast bar, a coffee in hand when I enter and reach for a bottle of water that I glug half down in one.

"You didn't want to join?" I ask, gesturing to the gym.

"Didn't want to interrupt," he corrects with a sleepy smile.

"Fair enough. Is everything okay?"

It may be like me to be up and moving in the early hours of the morning, and sometimes Jacob, too, when the nightmares gets too much, but not usually the rest of them. They sleep soundly and peacefully—something I can only dream of.

"Yeah, just my brain ticking over everything that's to come, you know?"

"I do. Is there anything I can help you with?"

It's been a busy week.

Once we decided on the university, there's been a flurry of decisions to make. This year or next? On site or off-site accommodation? Most importantly, how and where do we get one of those amazing group-sized beds? But with a little research, and a bit of common sense, we got there in the end. I think it's helped that we've had the celebration of life to coordinate, meaning we didn't have time or opportunity to overthink the whole thing. We'd make a decision, go with our guts, and move on. It may not work for every situation, but for these things, it has.

"Are you worried about the extra course?" I ask when he doesn't respond. "Because I've been trying to take that into consideration."

"If Nick can take one, I can," he says. "And didn't you find a house with spare for a couple of home offices? That would be really helpful."

Ivy fell in love with the cutest seafront terrace. Unfortunately, with no parking and spotty Wi-Fi connections, that was never going to be the one. Luckily for her, though, I found somewhere just ten minutes away, with enough space for Jacob's shoe collection, two home offices, and somewhere to stash the cars we'll need to take with us. Biggest bonus? It's a fifteen-minute drive to the sea. We can walk the seafront for a lazy evening stroll together, spend the day learning to surf with Wyatt, or just chill out and let Ivy catch up on her tan. All of which are perfect excuses to get half their clothes off, in my opinion.

"What happens afterwards?" he asks, drawing me in to the question I've been unable to answer thus far. "Nick is going to be a high-profile judge; he can't be linked to a poly relationship with a known underworld boss."

"It's a problem I've not got a solution for yet," I admit, glad I'm not the only one worrying about it. "He's going to be linked to me regardless, though, because of Jacob."

"So, even if we keep this relationship out of the limelight, it's going to be a problem. People are going to think he's corrupted... unscrupulous... dirty."

Footsteps sound out on the stairs, Jacob calling out, "Who's dirty?" before he appears in the doorway.

His brown hair sits in a sexy tousled mess on his head as he rubs the sleep from his eyes, taking in the two of us with a smirk. He pushes off the doorframe, trailing his fingers along the top of Wyatt's shoulders as a shiver of anticipation ripples through him from nothing more than a simple touch.

Rounding the breakfast bar, he places a quick kiss on the corner of my mouth, squeezing my dick through the soft fabric of my shorts as he reaches over for the coffee with his other hand.

"So, who's getting dirty, and how do I get in on this?" Jacob eventually asks, coffee in hand, clearly having missed most of our conversation.

"Leo's business dealings are dirty. How are we going to marry that up with mine and Nick's public personas?" Wyatt asks with a sigh, the seriousness of the discussion at hand knocking some of the flirtation right out of him.

"Let's worry about later problems later, shall we?" Jacob asks, resting back on the counter beside me and saying almost the exact same thing his twin did when I broached the subject with him. "The Sect seem to have a way to make what they want to happen a reality. Do you really not believe they could keep your reputation under wraps?" he asks, looking at me. "And do you not think there are ways to keep the public and the media away from our homes, from our lives? Come on, guys. This is a non-issue."

"Really?" Wyatt asks, his disbelief clear. "A non-issue?"

"We're through. We're safe," Jacob says, his tone implying something both of us have missed. "The Sect isn't going to let anything happen to us or our relationship The five of us are inextricably linked forever, or did you forget that?" he asks with the arch of an eyebrow and a tilt of his head.

We're a part of something now—something bigger than just the five of us—and it's permanent.

"I don't think anyone forgot that. I just never realised how far that might reach," I ponder, seeing the same thing dawning behind Wyatt's gaze.

"So, we just set up our own gated community and do whatever the hell we like, far away from the eyes of the public," Wyatt decides, wonder in his gaze.

"If that's what you want to do." Jacob shrugs, sipping his coffee. "Now, going back to this getting dirty… and adding in things you'd like to do… Wyatt, I've got a question for you." The mischievous twinkle in his eye should be a warning, but neither of us are prepared for the words that tumble out of his lips next.

"Have you ever kissed a guy?"

Wyatt's eyes widen in surprise, and I'm really glad his cup is empty, because I have a feeling both Jacob and I would be coated in coffee if it weren't.

"Uh… erm… No?" he blusters, the temperature in the room increasing by the second.

Dropping his forearms to the breakfast bar in front of Wyatt, Jacob places his mug between them, pressing his arse against my swelling dick as I get a front row seat to the interest playing in Wyatt's eyes.

"Do you want to?" Jacob asks, his tone sultry.

Wyatt has seemed happy just tagging in with Jacob and I here and there. He mostly sticks with Ivy. That's fine, whatever makes him happy, but it seems like Jacob wants to push the envelope this morning and see how far Wyatt might really like to take this newfound fascination.

"I, uh… I don't know," Wyatt replies, pressing his lips together, thoughts of it playing in those irises of his.

"Maybe he needs a demonstration?" I suggest, grinding myself against Jacob, the pressure boiling beneath my skin.

"He knows how to kiss; we've all seen him do it plenty of times. He's seen us kiss, too," Jacob says, looking at me over his shoulder. "You've sucked his cock, for God's sake, and I got my hands on that silky dick he hides away. It's beautiful, by the way," he adds, turning back to pin Wyatt with his intensity. "But I'm interested to know if there might be some reciprocation on the cards someday…"

I don't think he even realises he's doing it, but Wyatt's gaze flicks from Jacob's eyes to his lips, his tongue nipping out to wet his bottom lip before he presses them together, and there is nothing I can do to stop the swell of my cock. Just the memory of his lips around me is enough to have me hard, never mind when he does that.

Wyatt moves closer, adjusting his seat, his body moving without conscious thought when his gaze flicks to mine, his blush cuter than a button. But before he can find any words to respond with, the front door opens, the cleaning team arriving.

"Saved by the bell," Jacob says with a grin as he pops upright, giving both Wyatt and anyone who walks through the doorway a front row view of my hard on. "I'll be upstairs if anyone wants to join me," he says before filling his cup and sauntering back out like he didn't just breeze in here, solve a problem, and turn us both on in nothing more than minutes.

"He's just winding you up. You know there's no pressure to do anything you're not comfortable with, right?" I check, adjusting myself before the cleaners come in.

Wyatt swallows hard, watching the movement intently, which does absolutely nothing to help me will the damn thing away, but he nods nonetheless, clearly lost for words.

"I'm gonna go clean up. You coming?"

His panicked gaze finally leaves my crotch and meets my eyes, and suddenly, I hear the words that just tumbles out of my mouth.

"Uh, I mean, not coming-coming. Like, are you coming upstairs… not to help me shower… or you know… whatever," I rush out, attempting to explain myself, potentially only making it worse. "I'll just go... I'll see you in a bit."

I manage to get the words out in the right order and grab my bottle of water before scurrying away, but when I get to the relative safety of our bedroom, I realise we aren't the only ones Jacob's been winding up this morning. Nick's already two fingers deep in Ivy's sweet pussy.

Fuck, this is going to be a quick shower.

TWENTY-TWO

Ivy

"You know I'm starting this movie with or without you in ten minutes, right?" Leo asks, hovering in the doorway as I type away furiously.

"I know, I know. I just need to get this last bit done and then we're totally caught up," I reply, barely lifting my eyes from the screen.

I've been keeping mine and Jacob's sociology work ticking over, but doing it on my own has been harder than I anticipated. He's not quite caught up yet, but this will be the last assignment I have to do by myself... hopefully.

"I know he appreciates how hard you've worked on all this, but it will wait."

"I'll be done much quicker without you badgering me. Go make sure there are Maltesers, will you? I don't want to miss the start because I'm hunting down snacks."

"Or you could find them now... you know, before it starts?"

"Pleeeease?" I ask, giving him my best puppy dog eyes.

If I can get this finished, I'll be able to sit back and relax with everyone else, otherwise it's going to be humming away in the back of my mind all day.

His stare holds mine for the longest of seconds before breaking, a triumphant smile breaking free. "Fine, but you've got ten minutes, no more," he states, then turning and walking away.

Luckily, no one else decides to try and drag me away, and I make it to the end of the assignment, but not in the ten minutes I had left. I quickly press print before locking the computer and rushing downstairs, the house silent until I open the door to the movie room.

"Who are all these people, and what is going on?" I whisper-shout, attempting to make sense of what's happening on the screen as I slide into the closest seat next to Wyatt.

"Those are the security team. There's been a breach," he explains quietly.

"Why's she half-dressed?"

"I thought you'd seen this before?" he asks, pulling me in closer.

"I thought I had, too."

"Right, back it up, guys," Wyatt calls over the film. "Ivy's never seen it. We need to start over."

"It's five minutes in," Nick complains. "You've not missed anything major. You'll figure it out."

"Nope. Restart it. She needs all the background info from the beginning," Wyatt argues as the team on the screen make their way into a secret base.

"I warned you," Leo chides, tucking Jacob into his side.

"Really?" Nick grumbles, throwing a pointed look in Leo's direction before sighing and getting up. "Fine."

"There's popcorn and drinks on the side. I wasn't sure what you wanted," Leo says, throwing a bag of chocolates in my direction.

"I'm good with these for now but thank you."

"Did you get finished?" Jacob asks, shifting in his seat so he can see me better. "I'm pretty much there now, so we can adjust it together if that's okay?"

"Works for me," I reply with a shrug.

Having another pair of eyes on the work can only be a good thing, especially if those eyes know what they're looking for.

"Did you see the notes I left you for law?" Nick asks, the film all but forgotten as he picks up his popcorn and a cushion, throwing it on the floor in front of me before sitting and resting his head back against my skin.

"Yeah, that's going to take a touch longer to get up to date with, though. James is bringing the last of my history work over tomorrow and, as always, Leo has a plan," Jacob explains, running his fingers across Leo's chest.

He looks soft like this; gentle. When I dropped myself in Leo's lap back at the start of the year, there was something definitely dangerous about him. An edge. An aura. It's still there, sometimes. But now, he laughs, he smiles, he throws a mischievous wink towards Wyatt, and there's a whole lot of affection that wasn't there before.

But it's not just the soft smiles from Leo and the gentle exploration from Wyatt that's new. It's in the way that Nick is calmer, and Jacob is starting to open up to us all again. The safety we've all hid away from, frightened that it's nothing more than a fantasy, is here, it's ours, and it's finally starting to show.

The girls and I were locked in this room for hours whilst the Devils were out on a challenge. The challenge I thought Nick had lost, only to find out it was actually Jasper who didn't make it. This is the room where they broke George's leg, set out the rules of engagement, and confirmed that both Tamsin and Taylor were gone, amongst other things.

It doesn't exactly hold the fondest of memories for any of us, and yet here the five of us sit, talking about getting the jobs done and getting ready to move on to the next steps. Steps I thought had already been chosen, the decisions taken away from me, but that's not the case.

Coming here might have started with glasses breaking and alcohol sliding down the walls, but I'll be leaving with four men at my side who I would do anything for, who would do the same for me.

Four men I chose.

Men who love me, cherish me, and protect me.

We're walking out of here stronger than ever, with the backing of a society that will propel us forward, if only we knew what the price for that will be. How much of our souls will it cost to stay together?

Whatever it is, we'll pay it, because how could we not?

"Right, can we start this thing again now? There are five or six films, and they're not going to watch themselves," Nick gripes.

"Thank you," I whisper as he restarts it, running my fingers through the thick of his hair, my nails scraping against his scalp as my legs loop over Wyatt's.

And that's how we spend the next two days, cosied up

together, eating junk food, and watching zombie movies.
Like normal people.

TWENTY-THREE

Ivy

Six months later

The sun beats down against the sand, warming my skin, making everything else fade away into the distance. There are no rules, no exceptions, just the sun, the sand, and the next few hours laid out before us.

The peace won't last.

We're part of a secret society. There will always be expectations, but for now, we can forget about those and just be.

A cloud passes over, and my mind drifts, thinking back to the look on my mother's face when the guys turned up to collect my things ready for the move. I thought her eyes were going to pop out of her head when Nick and Jacob climbed out of the car, their matching dark jeans and light shirts hugging them both in all the right places.

Her gasp was audible when Leo strutted around the car, black on black, with ink crawling up his neck, giving him the ultimate bad-boy vibes. But it was when Wyatt appeared, pushing up the sleeves on his shirt and adjusting his aviators that I considered getting her a chair before she fainted. Her "Oh, my" wasn't missed by my father, either, and that did make me chuckle.

After all, wasn't he the one who dropped his only daughter consciously into the den of the Devils?

They all said their hellos and shook his hand. Jacob pressed a quick kiss to my cheek, but nobody else was quite so chaste. In fact, Nick's kiss was practically indecent, and I was both hot and flustered by the time we made it into the house, more than ready to ignore the boxes and say goodbye to my old life very rigorously and very loudly.

But they made it out unscathed, with my father fuming silently, even though he must have known I was tied to all three bloodlines. I guess it's different seeing it up close and personal.

"What are you smiling about?" Wyatt asks, dripping salt water on my overheated skin as he pulls his hair back, tying it up with a smirk. "Or maybe I shouldn't ask. This is a family friendly beach after all."

With a smile, I reply, "Oh, just you guys bowling my mother over."

"Good times." He nods, and I rest up on my forearms, following his line of sight to where Nick, Jacob, and Leo splash water at each other in the shallows.

"Why don't you join us?"

"That is going to get really scandalous really quickly," I say, eying up the water that drips down his chest with interest, his damp skin glistening in the sun.

"If you keep looking at me like that it will."

"And you think adding those three into the mix is going

to make it anymore PG? Maybe I should go find a wetsuit first—that might help."

He barks out a laugh, sliding his flip-flops off. "I don't think even that would stop them. It would just be more obvious to the rest of the world."

"Well, I think getting arrested for indecent exposure before we've even started is probably not the best idea. We'd better save those kinds of thoughts for when we get home."

"Sure. I'm going to suggest food shortly, just to warn you."

"Sounds good."

As if on cue, my stomach rumbles, definitely ready for something other than ice cream.

"Maybe sooner rather than later," he says. "I'll go grab them."

It's no hardship watching him jog the short distance to the water and call the guys back as all eyes turn to me. I'm sure the woman sitting just over from us isn't the only one distracted by all the rippling muscles, especially when her husband, boyfriend, or whoever coughs loudly to get her attention, causing even more of a stir.

I grab a couple of towels from the beach bag and pop them on the edge of my lounger before fishing around for my sun cream and dress. We've been out here for hours, and all that water is likely to have washed most of their sun protection off.

Damn it all, I'll have to slather their hot bodies in cream again. Such a hardship.

It takes barely fifteen minutes to get everyone dry and

topped up. I've barely thrown my dress on when Leo packs up the last of our stuff and takes my hand, following Nick and Jacob up the steps and onto the boardwalk.

"Do you want to grab something now, or one of us can cook when we get back?" Leo asks.

"It's too hot to cook," I grumble, not ready to step back into the beautiful but way too warm kitchen of our new home.

"You know what I haven't had in forever? A bag of chips and bits," he declares excitedly, spotting something up ahead.

"That sounds disgusting," Nick gripes, not even turning around.

"Oh, man. You don't know what you're missing," Wyatt argues. "Let's find a chippy. That sounds perfect."

"What are these *bits* of?" Jacob asks warily, stealing the question straight out of my mouth.

"They're like little fried bits of batter soaked in salt and vinegar, then scattered in a huge pile of chips. Delicious," Leo explains.

"Sounds like a heart attack waiting to happen," Nick complains.

"Don't knock it 'til you've tried it," Leo counters.

"I used to love a bag of those after a good session on the waves," Wyatt agrees.

"So, it's like a tradition, then? I guess that means we have to," Jacob says, looking over his shoulder to catch Wyatt's gaze with a wink.

"You want some Nick, or shall I just see if they can throw a salad together for you?" Leo asks sarcastically.

With some grumbling, Nick agrees to give them a try, and Leo and Jacob head over to order while the three of us loiter against the wall to wait.

"Next time, we should bring some boards," Nick suggests absentmindedly while watching the rolling waves, the heat of his body pressing against mine as he drops his arm over my shoulders.

"We'll need a rack for the car before we manage that," Wyatt says, and the two of them fall into conversation about surf boards, parking, and logistics.

Before they get to the end of it, Leo and Jacob are back, with trays of chips covered in batter bits stacked in their hands.

"Moment of truth," Wyatt jokes, watching Nick's reaction with interest.

"I don't know why you're all looking at me like that. It's fine. Nothing super amazing, but it's edible, I suppose," Nick declares with a shrug of his shoulders.

"Great praise indeed," Jacob says with a smirk.

We pick up our things and continue meandering, chatting, and eating, the greasy food hitting the spot perfectly.

"Does this bring back fond memories of home for you both?" I ask, looking at Wyatt and Leo.

"Oh, absolutely," Wyatt agrees, shoving another forkful in his mouth.

"The afternoons we managed to escape my father and grab a bag of these to share, sitting in the grass in the park… those were the best," Leo says with a nod.

"We?"

"Dex and Blaise. They're my brothers. Not by blood, but in all the ways that matter," he clarifies.

"Are those the guys Ruby has a thing for? The one in the black car?" I ask.

"Didn't know she had a thing for him," he replies, eyebrows rising in interest. "But, yes. Dex drives the car."

"Dex… Hmm, okay. I'll file that name away for the next time I speak to her. She's still totally denying it, but it's obvious if you ask me."

"Good to know." He nods, pondering. "Anyway, the three of us have been friends forever. They're the ones who were sending the hints to the house: the quiz book, the flowers… and they're the ones who were keeping an eye on Jacob whilst he was… away."

"Did they ever tell you what they did?" Jacob asks, his steps faltering for a second.

"No, I left it with them, knowing they'd do only what was safe to do. If I knew what you were going through and what they had to help with, I'm reasonably sure I'd have said fuck it all and stormed in there to get you," Leo admits, a blush rising on his cheeks.

"Sophie and Carlos never told us, either," Nick admits. "The radio silence was absolute torture but, again, there's a good chance we'd have been making moves we shouldn't have done if we'd known how you got those, and whose face needed breaking for them," he says, gesturing to Jacob's back.

The marks have healed well over the last few months, but despite the heat of the day, he's got them covered. It didn't stop him from stripping down to his shorts to jump in the waves, but he did cover up when he came back to the beach with me. I think the kisses Leo places on them every night and the oil Wyatt put together for him are both helping, but it's a process.

"One day," Jacob promises. "One day, I'll tell you, and one day we'll take the blood you're picturing. Just... not yet."

We fall silent, everyone finishing their food as we make our way back to the car, load up, and head home.

"So, can we take part in Freshers' Week?" Jacob asks as the front door closes behind us, apparently ready for a more positive conversation.

"My father said to keep our noses clean—no trouble, and to keep in touch—so I can't see why not," Wyatt says, taking the bags through to the laundry. "I'm sure a week of partying is exactly what he had in mind."

"I was told to keep my ear to the ground," Leo adds, pulling a handful of beers from the fridge. "I think that means we should. How else are we going to know what's going on?"

"Exactly. We need to make some friends and be in the thick of it. Let's just not stick out and make a mess?" Wyatt suggests, coming back in and pressing his lips to Jacob's.

"I think the five of us turning up anywhere is going to turn a few heads," I comment, dropping onto the sectional and thinking about how oblivious we are to the sexuality that oozes from our dynamic.

The five of us finding our rhythm has taken a minute, or two. Wyatt has stepped into his sexuality in a big way, opening doors with both Leo and Wyatt, but never too far from me either. Nick still only has eyes for me, but letting his guard down and opening his heart to Wyatt and Leo has been a process just as important.

Jacob returning showed us all just how much we need each other, sexually, emotionally, mentally. We're a unit. Until death. And nobody will come between us again.

Wyatt snuggles into the corner, pulling me into his side as Nick drops his legs over the arm rest, his feet hanging over the edge, with his head landing gently in my lap. Leo hands out the beers, and Jacob joins on the other side of Wyatt, with Leo settling on his other side just as the credits roll.

"Good point, but there's not much we can do about that," Jacob decides.

And so, the five of us settle into our new house by the sea, free from our overbearing parents, with minimal instructions from The Sect, but a big list of things to be done.

If we thought that coming away to university was going to be something like a break, we were wrong. On the plus side, we're together, and we're moving up in the world. One step at a time.

TWENTY-FOUR

Ruby

It's funny the things you notice when no one is watching you.

Like Leo. He used to be cold and closed-off. A dark aura with a spiky disposition. At least he was with me when we were first introduced at Ivy's pool house spa day. But now, some six months later, he's smiling, happy, and joking with a friend without a care in the world.

How? Why?

Is this what happens when you find safety and security? Or is it because of Ivy? Because of them?

I understand the draw to it: the darkness. Not Leo—never him but the pull to something dangerous? That, I understand.

That exposure got me in trouble once before. Well, at least once, until I was saved by someone unexpected and closer to home than he should have been.

I shouldn't be attracted to him. Seeing firsthand what he's capable of most definitely shouldn't have been a turn on, but I've never seen or felt anything like it.

His safety, his warmth, the barely-laced fury he unleashed on those unsuspecting idiots. I've never forgotten it, and my infatuation only seems to be growing.

But watching Leo slip out of the back doors of the party, I know *he's* out there. Hiding. Waiting. Becoming the darkness he wholly embodies.

The question is, is he here for Leo… or for me?

ACKNOWLEDGMENTS

Wyatt – Well, finally I managed to get a word in on one of these damn books. Of course it was only one chapter, and the one where you're practically carving my soul out. Bloody author. But at least the readers got a little peek into how my brain works. In case you didn't figure it out yet, I'm the one holding it all together-

Nick – Yeah, right. Or so you'd like to think.

Wyatt – I would, actually. Some of us aren't roaming around causing a ruckus, we're just working with the hand we've been played, quietly and meticulously in the background.

Leo – If you two are finished bickering the rest of us might like to say something? Done? Right, great. Well, I feel like I am the luckiest son of a bitch in the world right now. I've got the man I wanted on one arm, the woman I wanted on the other arm, the sun on my face, and someone else that crept up on me. Someone that I never in a million years considered would be interested, and yet, he's looking at me like he's ready to devour me. Yeah, that last one's not Nick, just for reference.

Nick – Not happening, bro. We've been through this. Meta-whore's for life.

Jacob – Yeah, that's not what it's called and you fucking know it. Anyway, we just wanted to jump in before the author starts her boring ramble about all the people that propped her up throughout this journey to say thanks. Thanks for taking the prequel of two brothers and two strangers. Guys that were bloody, beaten, and confused, and running with us through all the chaos that ensued.

Nick – And there's been plenty of chaos. Okay, I admit it, some of it was by my hand, but with the best of intentions. Only ever the best intentions for you guys

Ivy – So, yeah. Thanks for being here, thanks for sticking it out. Uni is going to be a whole other kind of adventure and open up doors for us all, and we can't wait to start. Oh, and don't miss out on catching up with my girl Ruby in her book. That dark mysterious driver of hers has some secrets to tell, I'm sure.

Thanks guys, for chipping in as always. I guess it means that it's my turn now, the author.

So, thanks for being here, the readers. Thanks for taking a risk on an author you might not have read before and a series that started off slow burn and got hot, and especially thanks for trusting me through the process as we went from book to book.

As always, a massive thank you must go to my husband, the one who said I'd go this far even when I didn't believe him. The one who has supported me every step of the way. To Donna, Angela, Karen and Christina for your unwavering encouragement and support, you guys have always got my back.

And always to Vicki and Lou for their work in prepping my messy, gone over it twenty-four million times but it's still not quite got it right document. For their late night questions, refinement, adjustment, teaching and friendship. It means more than you know.

Heather x

About the Author

HL Packer is quite frankly, a busy bee.

When she's not running around after her free-spirited three children, and husband. You can find her tending to the dogs, bearded dragons, and snakes that also reside with them.

When she finished her office job for maternity leave, her husband purchased a Kindle E-Reader to give her something to do, and oh what a journey that has been. From reading to reviewing, then blogging and creating Romance Readers Book Box UK. And now, her own words being put out into the world.

When she is not coordinating her worlds, you can find her soaking in a bubbly bath or enjoying a glass of wine, often still with a book in her hand.

Newsletter: https://bit.ly/3rdYAny

Also by H.L. Packer

Fated Series

Home

Within Reach

Within Hope

The Shadow

Amore

La Familglia

The Ties that Bind

The Bonds That Break

Broken Lies

Fractured Truth

Pendleton Prep

The Sect

Her Devil

His Angel

Their Hell

Our Heaven

www.ingramcontent.com/pod-product-compliance
Lightning Source LLC
Chambersburg PA
CBHW031323210726

48287CB00005B/1659